SHARK CHUTNEY

SHARK CHUTNEY

A TALE FROM A SHIFTING SHORE

a novella

VIKRAM GREWAL

First published by NU VOICE PRESS 2025
An imprint of Hubhawks Pvt. Ltd
www.nuvoicepress.com

This is a work of fiction and all characters and incidents described in this book are the product of the author's imagination. Any resemblance to actual persons, living or dead, is entirely coincidental.

ISBN: 978-81-988726-4-7

Printed at Thomson Press India Ltd.
Published by: Nu Voice Press

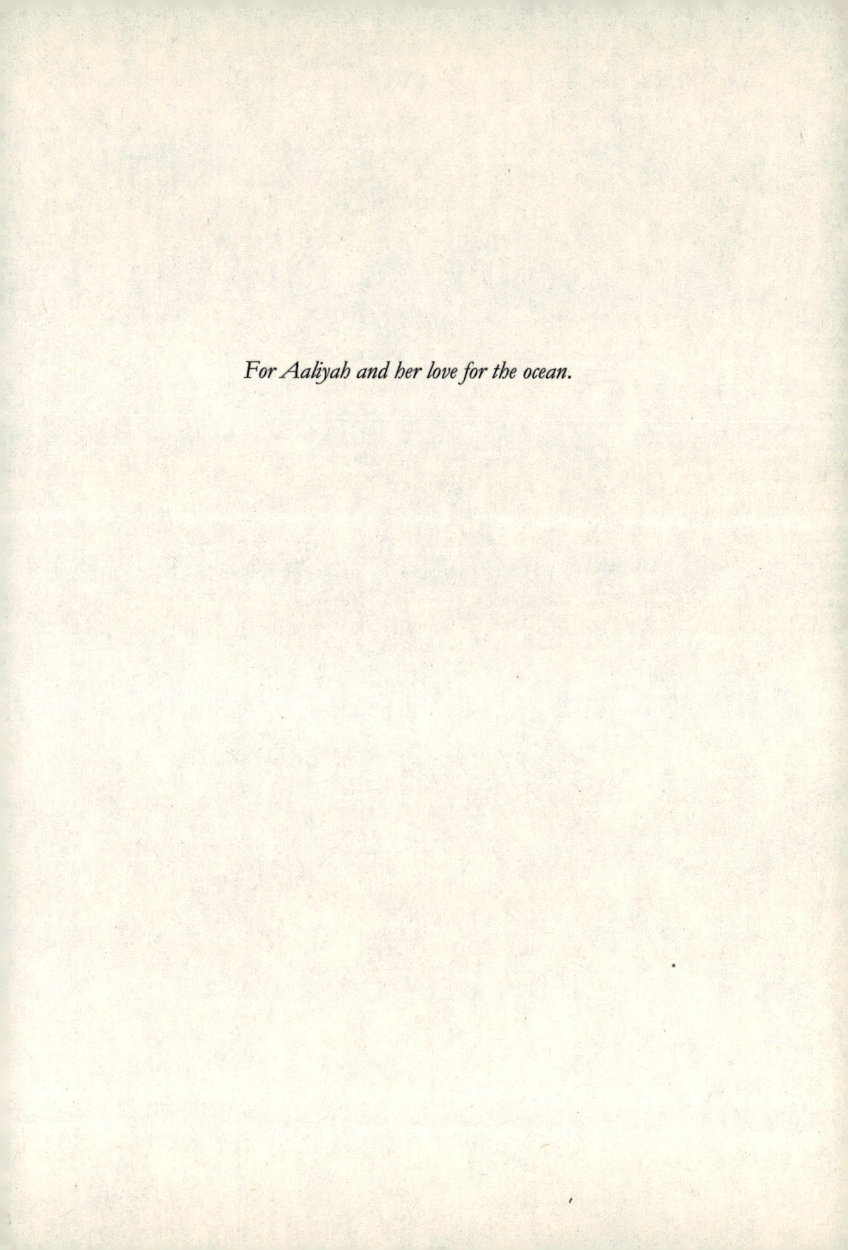

For Aaliyah and her love for the ocean.

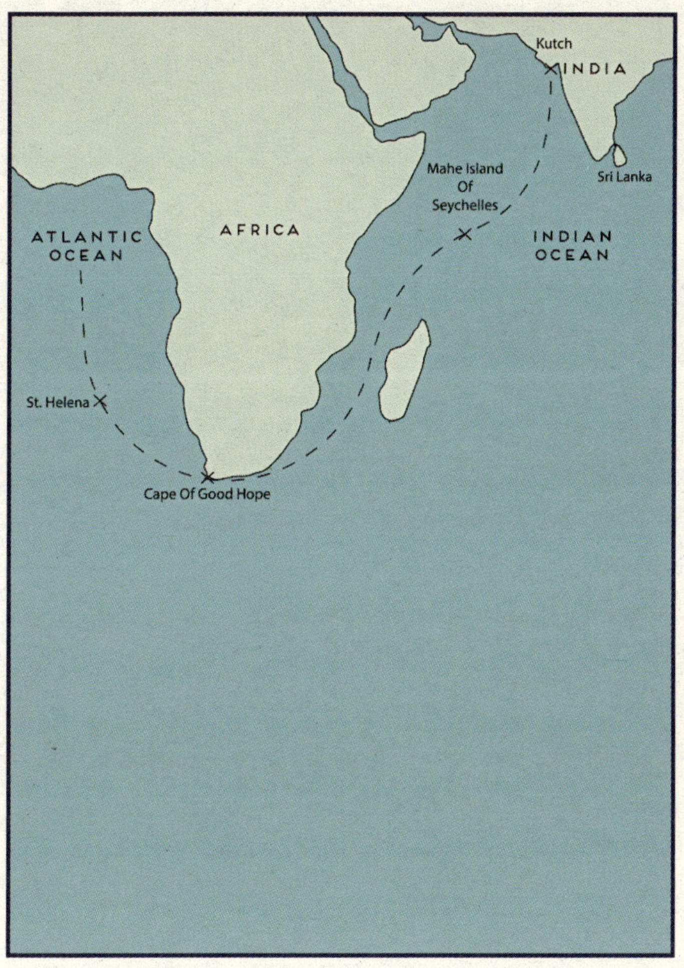
Kutch
INDIA
Sri Lanka
Mahe Island
Of
Seychelles
AFRICA
ATLANTIC
OCEAN
INDIAN
OCEAN
St. Helena
Cape Of Good Hope

AUTHOR'S NOTE

Consider this work as a documentary fable, for it is a surrealistic representation of real occurrences. It is a fictionalized retelling of incidents that happened on the island of Mahé in the Seychelles archipelago between May 2022 and May 2024. The demonym for people from Seychelles is 'Seychellois' in English and 'Seselwa' in the native Creole language. The author has chosen to use the latter to save ink.

The author takes full responsibility of all the *greegree* that adorns these pages and declares that the views expressed do not reflect the opinion of any human or suprahuman entity, because what follows is merely magic, in black and white and sepia.

V.G.
March 2025

CONTENTS

DAVVN

JONATHAN STARED AT the rising sun, not knowing what it actually looked like. His eyes had been foggy with cataracts and his nose lay dormant to smell for decades now. He did feel that he had seen and smelt enough, though. A life that would seem long enough to anyone who breathed on this land. He was nearing two hundred—the oldest of all the living land animals.

He peeped out of his shell steadily and looked at the luminous aura on the horizon. Each dawn on the island of Saint Helena, the sun's rays would greet him as if bringing him a message from home. Home that lay on the other side of the continent—in the Indian Ocean. Jonathan was born in the archipelago of Seychelles a decade after Napoleon Bonaparte died on the island of Saint Helena. He was forced to travel across from the Indian Ocean and onto the Atlantic—from the middle of nowhere in one ocean, to the middle of nowhere in another ocean.

Jonathan had lived through time as an aloof spectator. He had lived through the world wars, the great depressions, the famines, and the pandemics without complaining even once. His ignorance was a function of geographical nicety and boring privilege. He had comfortably spent more than a century munching on his greens and mating with various, perpetually younger mates on the lawns of the Governor's plantation house.

He was a state symbol of heritage and conservation, a living amalgamation of nature and history. He had had the best life could offer, and in fact, the most it could offer. Yet, each dawn he looked at the red blip far into the ocean turn orange and yellow. His foggy eyes still had dreams and aspirations to be somewhere else—at home.

He remembered seeing a green turtle once, a hundred years back. He had looked into his eyes through the glass container that held the rescued turtle and felt that he was looking at a mirror. But as the turtle swam swiftly along the edge, Jonathan realized his slow neck and body were not as blessed with agility. Thereafter, during such dawns, he remembered this encounter and dreamt of being more than an immortal state refugee living thousands of miles away from home. Jonathan the tortoise dreamt of being a turtle someday. Jonathan the tortoise dreamt of going home.

1

THE MEN

I

THIS HAPPENED on the first Wednesday in the month of May.

It happened to be the first day of the month as well. It also happened to be the only month of twenty-twenty-four to start on a Wednesday. Moreover, it happened to be the only public holiday falling on a Wednesday that year—apart from Christmas. But Christmas happened to be two weeks long in the Seychelles, so Wednesday didn't seem to make any difference in that case. However, Wednesday—the first of May in the lord's third millennium and twenty-four—was special. Because this happened on a Wednesday that felt very much like a Sunday.

The first of May was more like Sunday than Sunday itself for the people of the island of Mahé—which happens to be the largest of the one hundred and fifteen islands of the archipelago of Seychelles. And Seychelles happens to be the only inhabited country settled on granitic islands in the world. And it is right in the middle of nowhere—if nowhere happens to be somewhere in the Indian Ocean.

And everywhere in this island grows the Red Lady in its full glory. The Red Lady is the keeper of time. On a land surrounded by bodies of water on all sides for millions of years, time—as we know it—could never reach. In the hinterland, time was governed first by one lone brick in the sun, then two halves of an hourglass, then three hands of a clock and so on. However, none of them could swim across to touch the virgin sands of Mahé—until the Red Lady arrived. She came riding the fruit bats from Southern Africa, leaving her ancestors behind in the New World of Americas where they had been domesticated by the conquistadors. In no time, she had spread her juicy highness from one end of the island to the other.

The Red Lady kept time faithfully. Monday, green she fell. Tuesday, she was emerald. Wednesday, she was olive. Thursday, she was yellow. Friday, she was mustard. Saturday, she was pink. Sunday, she was red—and cut to bits. For that was the cycle of the best papayas in the world! To see them ripen through the week and let them be the perfect breakfast before Sunday mass. The Red Lady papayas, almost singlehandedly, brought routine in the random lives of the people of Seychelles. The cutting of one Red Lady marked the end of one week. An average person lived up to four thousand Red Ladies while the oldest tortoise on the island was over ten thousand Red Ladies old.

In twenty-twenty-four, the first of May brought collective panic in the minds of many Seselwa people—it felt like Sunday! A premature Sunday had arrived after two days from the last Sunday. It was a holiday, so all the shops and offices were closed. And all Red Ladies on the island, which were otherwise supposed to be olive, had turned red that morning!

The head priests of all the local chapels were woken up by the incessant ringing of their phones. People were calling to ask if there was Sunday mass on a Wednesday since the

Red Ladies had indicated divine will for a mid-week congregation. 'It is Labor Day for God's sake!' they replied, and hung up to nurse their hangovers from the previous night of Walpurgis which was marked by a special catholic mass till midnight. This was followed by the booze party to welcome May Day—a festival that brought with it a new month's salary to be splurged merrily. When the Victoria Clock Tower struck twelve, a group of noisy pick-up trucks drove around the centre of the only cross-road of the country. This circumambulation lasted less than a minute, as the passengers had important business to attend to at the island casino, leaving the lone heritage Clock Tower standing in the middle of a deserted capital of a nation in celebration.

Labor Day was inarguably the favourite holiday of the people of Seychelles, primarily because it was the very first day of the month and workers were given their salaries afresh in addition to the day-off (which was solemnly spent sucking on lime and lemons to cure migraines from the alcohol that flowed into their guts on the last day of April). And Labor Day falling on a Wednesday meant that a week had been effectively halved by the Almighty to mark the union of the maypole with the hammer and the sickle. Some drunk workers thought that the Red Ladies turning red on Labor Day was evidence enough to demonstrate God's socialism. Seated in La Dolce Vita—the only restaurant open that morning in the capital city Victoria, the tourists from Russia poured more vodka in their glasses to celebrate and the tourists from France clinked red wine flutes and cried 'chin chin!' The rest of Victoria was as quiet as her secret.

The people of Seychelles take their holidays very seriously. They strictly subject themselves to extended bouts of relaxation and merriment. Work is prohibited and there is an unsaid covenant amongst all to not be available for any task that may be avoidable or unavoidable. A policy of non-discrimination is followed when it comes to classifying chores—all of them are equally secondary. Rest is primary: a lazy morning (if there is one), a late afternoon (if the morning survives), a slow evening (which is still after noon) and an endless night (that ends five minutes before workplaces open the next day).

There are no hours or minutes or seconds on Mahé since the Red Ladies can only keep time in a weekly fashion. A 'week' is the fundamental unit of time on the island—not seconds. A bill is due every two or four weeks. An official meeting is tentatively fixed for a certain week. The grocery store refuels its stock from the wholesaler depending on the weekly demand, and the fruits and vegetable market work on a weekly basis. Chickens are brought to the butcher once a week and eggs are collected from the hatchery once a week. Chopping of mutton, lamb, beef, and pork is miniscule, since most of it is imported, weekly. No cereals are grown on the island as these follow seasonal cycles unlike the gourds that dominate local produce thanks to their weekly progression of growth—a week of sowing, two weeks of ventilated shade before transplantation, and then four weeks of nurturing, and three weeks of waiting.

The premature redness of the Red Ladies had disrupted the island clock. The usual calm of a holiday had been replaced by pandemonium in all neighbourhoods. What did it mean, the reddening? Were the Gods angry with the Seselwa? Was this a warning? An omen of impending doom?

Would all papayas start turning red suddenly without reaching their ripe states? Had this happened elsewhere too? Did this mean these fruits were poisonous? Curiosity and inquisitiveness were not really traits of the island folk, but this anomaly had ripped right through space and time.

A local headmaster posted on the Gossip Corner, 'It was never the apple in the Eden! Eve plucked a papaya! A red one. And she turned red after eating that forbidden fruit. God was angry with her and turned her into a papaya herself. That is why we call it the "Red Lady!" And this happened on a Wednesday—millions of years ago! And today, history has come to repeat itself. Lord be merciful! We are in the end of days. Pray, dear people! Pray to our Lord! Stay home and pray for your children! Let's all ask for strength. Amen.'

Gossip Corner is a Facebook group with the tagline 'Keeping it real since 2011' where gossip from all across the one hundred and fifteen islands of the Seychelles accumulates. This post received five likes and three comments—which, for a country of just a hundred thousand people, meant that it had gone viral. It was enough to impose a state of spiritual emergency!

A country with less land has more time. There is only so far you could go, and only so much you could do. A moment of eternity hit your face each day twice—once with the sea breeze during the day and another with the land breeze at night. It was the breeze that regulated the existence of the island standing tall in the middle of so much water. It was the breeze that acted as the language between the one hundred islands of solitude. The breeze was to the islands what gossip was to its inhabitants.

The breeze had reddened the papayas before due time, like the gossip that had now reddened the white, black, brown, and yellow faces of the people of Mahé. 'It was a divine test,' the folks said. A test of our solidarity amidst increasing diversity. Seychelles hosted almost equal populations originating from Africa, Europe, and Asia who had assimilated with the mélange milieu that had thrived on these islands since their first habitation in the late eighteenth century. African, British, French, Indian, and Chinese cultures had been ground well by the forces of time that added them to the base of Malagasy and Creole demography to produce a beautiful, harmonious, and delicious *chutney* of plurality. And after gaining independence from the British colonizers in the late twentieth century, Seychelles expanded its horizons as a tourist country welcoming Russian, Arab, and Australian settlers who chose to stay on long after their originally-planned short visits to these paradisical islands.

'Too many colors mess up the canvas,' a politician with speculative interest in art had once posted on the Gossip Corner when immigration issues and racial diversity were becoming hot topics for the upcoming elections. The Seselwa people looked at the question of race very differently from the hinterland. For a civilization that had commenced on the basis of pluralism and organic assimilation, discrimination on the basis of color and ethnicity seemed incomprehensible at first. However, as these so-called 'virgin islands' embraced the so-called impure complexities of the globalized world, concocted perceptions and political biases made a smooth entry onto its beaches by floating along the breeze that brushed the islands' granite faces ominously.

The first of May had too many firsts for an island used to being last when it came to the pace of life and the scale of happenings born of happenstance. The unnatural reddening of the Red Ladies was not really a spiritual chaos in reality, but what could one expect from half-asleep staunch believers on a mid-week holiday, half-drunk on rum and half-drunk on religion. Here, rum and religion were exports initially, but over time Seychelles had learnt to brew, distil, mix and sell both as per their need and ability. Today, the country boasts of the highest rate of consumption of alcohol per capita—to which tourism might be a huge contributor as well. The annual tourist footfall is three times the size of its population.

The Red Ladies were an ecological indicator, not a spiritual or a political one. It neither reflected the end of days, nor did it mean that the demography was acting up due to its diversity. This was pointed out in very plain words by the ecologist at the local university—who, unlike the school teacher harking on religious instruction and the politician mincing art and ideology, was doing exactly what she was supposed to do. She wrote on the Gossip Corner, 'Climate is changing. This does not stop at the papayas.' She made sense, the young students thought for a minute, and then continued to enjoy their off day on social media, gulping down freshly cut Red Ladies on a Wednesday.

To have opinions and media for their expression was a privilege and function of time. Most islanders seemed to have it. But for some, who still did not consider themselves as islanders—or rather, were not allowed to consider themselves as residents of Mahé, it was distant and difficult. And among them, were the workers of the Gangwani estate—a ten-acre fruit and vegetable farm at the southern tip of the island, where the first of May did not mean anything different from any other day. The workers had never even heard of 'Labor Day' before coming to Seychelles. They had never seen or tasted a Red Lady before their arrival here.

And on this estate, the morning of that Wednesday alarmed all eighteen workers—except Hitesbhai, who knew that time was now changing indeed. And it wouldn't stop at the papayas.

II

HITESBHAI 'MALBA' THAKO had been a salt farmer with a sweet tooth. The locals had given him the middle name *Malba* which was the middle name given to all South Asians, mostly Indians, living in Seychelles by default. It was derived from the term 'Malabar' referring to the south-western coast of India which was a gateway to the Indian Ocean since time immemorial. Many thought of it as a derogatory term as it almost sounded like the word for 'debris' or 'waste' in Hindi. However, Hitesbhai thought of it as an endearing salutation compared to how his own villagers treated him back in his hometown in Kutch, the salt-basket of India. They never called him or his family anything. They merely used the clicking of the tongue or smacking of the lips to make strange sounds—to which Hitesbhai had been trained to respond over the years.

His mother called him *misri* or sugar crystal because of his deep love for sweet things. She could never pronounce 'sh' in '*mishri*' and that is also why he was named 'Hites' and not 'Hitesh.' He could only complete primary school where he learned how to pronounce his own name correctly. He would tell his mother about the discrepancy—that his name only started with an 'h' and did not end with one. She would anyway continue to call him '*misri*.' He repeatedly told the same thing to his fellow workers on Mahé too—but very few cared about his name or its pronunciation, as he was just 'Malba' at the end of the day—and even at its beginning.

The beginning of May had not surprised Hitesbhai. In fact, he had forgotten the sensation of surprise altogether since leaving home. Surprises were never kind, he thought. They were insensitive and selfish—like Hittalbhai Pandya who had sold off his salt farm to buy a ticket to America. He had left without even informing his workers, which included Hitesbhai's parents among a dozen others. That surprise shook numerous families in the village. Some of them were never seen again.

But now Hites was an 'expat'—a word he learnt at the reception of the embassy in Victoria a year back. He had gone to deliver some papaya saplings for a tree plantation drive. The saplings died in a week and were forgotten but the word 'expat' stuck to his brain like the Praslin snail on a Takamaka tree. The idea of a tree plantation drive on a tropical island kissing the equator seemed to be absurd. It was indeed absurd to the several generations of Seselwa who had lived on this paradise of an island enjoying all its divine blessings, thanks to a ubiquitous thick canopy: pure oxygen, clean water, natural produce, delicious fruits, and heavenly breeze. With sporadic shipments of cereals added to this, there was enough for everyone's need. However, as the tourism moguls kept arriving in Victoria and as the fish market began expanding and land began to be reclaimed from the ocean to create pockets of estates along the coast, a need for hard working labor was realized on a national scale to regularize and capitalize resources. The tropical jungle had to make way for some disciplined tree columns and the tiny state capital had to make way for big office buildings. And in came thousands of expats like Hitesbhai and his Gangwani comrades! They were the foot soldiers of development in the country—that happened to be not their own.

Mahé had been a microcosm of human civilization attempting to tame nature since its discovery and settlement. That may be a discussion for subsequent papaya cuttings, but one thing was quite conspicuous—the laid-back pace of the island was in confrontation with the capitalistic rat race that was coming through its shores from the outside world. For the ordinary Seselwa, work was unnatural and antithetical to continued existence that hinged on simple living and slow growth. It was normal for people to live up to a hundred years in the archipelago. No wonder their national animal is the tortoise—slow, satisfied, wise, and relatively immortal!

The concept of 'work' has a different meaning for island dwellers as compared to 'continental' dwellers. It is just like its geography—limited, isolated, and enough. Work is neither identity nor necessity. There was an attorney at the Supreme Court who was also a property agent, a saxophonist in a local band, and ran a yogurt business in the same neighborhood as a whistler who drank all day and screamed all night at each passing vehicle—both best of friends (being a 'whistler' here involves whistling alone and nothing subsidiary). Their work didn't define or divide them. Neither did it occupy the same significance in people's minds. It makes no difference if you do three jobs between nine to five or none. If you are making ends meet or ends are making you meet. Mahé has enough for mankind—

thanks to a robust expat cheap labor force that is ever-ready to leave their homelands and reach these shores.

Hitesbhai and his family had to leave the salt farm in the deserted and deserted lakes of Kutch after they were deserted by the owner Hittalbhai who sold it off for moving to the United States, just before the coronavirus pandemic struck—fortunately for the latter landlord and unfortunately for the former farmer. After two years of grappling with the perceived end of the world, an opportunity came calling for the Thako family. A local agent informed them that Waro Company was hiring young, able-bodied farm laborers in Seychelles and that Hites would fit the bill, but a passport would be needed. Hearing this, all of them smiled with desperation, however, they had two questions: 'Where is a passport?' and 'What is a Seychelles?'

On the fourth of May, Hitesbhai would complete two years of his contract with Waro Company. That would be in three days. All the eighteen workers of Gangwani Estate would then be exchanged with the twenty workers on Esomption Estate, which lay about a thousand miles to the west. Hitesbhai loved being with all the seventeen fellow farm laborers in his company. Five of them were from Bangladesh, four from Pakistan, three from Sri Lanka, two from Nepal, and the rest from India. All of them had arrived in Mahé two years back. In the first six months, all of them had decided to end the contract and return home. The island had given them a cultural shock: roads were empty, homes were sparse, women were outspoken, and there were no onions. Shipments had become too erratic because of high freight charges during the pandemic. This meant irregular supply of potatoes and diminishing supply of onions—both were essential for the subcontinental appetite that the Gangwani Estate now sported.

The unavailability of onions and potatoes were not a problem for Hitesbhai whose salty appetite and sugary desire had been a frugal spectrum when it came to cuisine. Onion and garlic were rarely used in his village in Kutch. Mahé seemed like an island of abundance to him. The local produce of golden apple, starfruit, banana, and papaya had come across to him as a blessing. He had never seen such a lush regular harvest of fruit from where he had come. He had definitely tasted mangoes in India—his sweetest memory—but it made him sad knowing that the season of mangoes lasted for only a couple of months each year and even the rich could not make them grow beyond that for themselves. He had even seen Hittalbhai trying to get crates and crates of mangoes delivered from other states, but all of them went rotten a month after the end of monsoon. However, in Mahé, mangoes were undomesticated and had three seasons of four months each, which meant they were always ready to be plucked. After getting to know this, Hitesbhai was sure that Mahé was paradise. In the very first month of his arrival, he ate so many mangoes that he fell sick. Chetty Papa made him a special spicy onion stew for a week which brought him back to health. That is when Hitesbhai realized the importance of onions—and of Chetty Papa.

When the newly arrived Gangwani Eighteen conveyed their dissatisfaction over the food given to them, Chetty Papa was quick to respond, 'Cook yourself!' They grew the produce on the estate anyway, he said, might as well start making your own food. This would allow the mess staff to be shifted to another estate thus saving some money that could be put in to buy the high-priced onion and potato shipments from the market. And as for the spices, Chetty Papa would get them from his own grocery store near English River. Consensus was immediately reached and the mess staff dispatched. The Gangwani Eighteen, thereby, began enjoying the fruits of their own labor.

Hitesbhai's labor for growing fruits was a labor of love. He learnt each day from Chetty Papa, the chief caretaker of the estate, who was a fourth generation migrant Seselwa. His family had shifted from the sugar plantations of Mauritius to Seychelles at the beginning of the previous century. Since then, they were a farming and trading community under the protection of the Waro family. Chetty Papa taught Hitesbhai all about fruits: breadfruit, starfruit, passionfruit, jackfruit, dragon fruit, and all other local fruits that did not have 'fruit' in their names, yet were fruitier. The fruitiest of all fruits were the Red Ladies. Hitesbhai fell in love with them instantly.

It was love at first bite. Hitesbhai had heard of papayas earlier and had even seen one at a juice corner in the city of Ahmedabad from where he had to catch a train to Mumbai, but he had never tasted one. Before he could taste the first papaya of his life, he had to take the first train of his life to take the first flight of his life. It was his first trip outside his state as well as outside his country—all within a matter of twenty-two hours. Those twenty-two hours of the year twenty-two made him feel nervous and scared looking at the alien glass buildings and steel chariots of a big city. He ate the staple meal of three salted *puris* with mango pickle that his mother had packed for the journey on the Surya Nagari express—'the Golden City express.' He reached Mumbai before mid-day, but only at night did he notice that the city was actually golden. With tarmacs reflecting yellow street lamps, the city was glistening in sepia. It reminded him of the colors of the salt farm at sunset in his village when the red light kissed the white mounds of salt and scattered in similar sepia. He thought of his 'golden' village looking at the golden city as the aircraft took off and made its way across the Indian Ocean and towards the middle of nowhere. He did not blink on the flight out of the fear of falling off into the darkness below. This fear, coupled with a serious bout of jet lag, persisted for a few days after reaching Mahé. Hitesbhai did not know what jet lag was, but he certainly knew the feeling of homesickness. The Red Lady came as remedy first, love came a little later perhaps.

It was his first Sunday on Mahé when Hitesbhai was given a Red Lady to cut. It was golden and full. It was soft and firm. It was light and heavy. It was like a fistful of salt at sunset. It was perfect. He knew he was holding something more than a papaya. This was not ordinary. This was a divine blessing. It was not a produce from man, he thought, it was crafted by the goddess herself. Her village goddess who would turn all things to gold—just like how she had been turning the salt farms around his village from white to golden yellow forcing the farm owners to sell and leave for greener pastures. The Red Lady was the opposite of this and hence, enticing in that regard. It turned green to gold from the outside and reddish pink from the inside. Hites made slow, gentle cuts with the blunt wooden knife that Chetty Papa had thrown at him (sure of the knife being harmless, he did occasionally throw it onto the workers at Gangwani). As he carved long boomerangs from the pink fleshy fruit sitting under its tree, he felt like he was peeling the Earth from the surface to the core. And as he scooped out the seedy centre, he felt like he was disembowelling the whole planet—like his village goddess. He took the black seeds, in his palm wet with papaya juice, and squeezed them dry. Exposing them to seething sunlight he desiccated them for a few minutes and then violently threw them in the air—they scattered like villagers fleeing for survival. In this moment of ecstasy, Hites passionately butchered the fruit and devoured it like a hungry madman—his eyes, nose, cheeks, and lips all smeared with red and pink pulp. This was the sweetest thing he had ever eaten. He cried and tried—to push his head into the leftover half of the fruit, searching for a portal inside that may take him back to Kutch, to his village, to his family. The Red Lady, in all its fleshy smithereens, embraced his face with pink warmth like a parent hugging a long-lost child. He tasted his own salty tears mixed with the sweet pulp of the papaya. It was the mix of salt and sugar that made him feel closer to his village community kitchen where Gujarati cuisine was made on special occasions and all the dishes were both sweet and salty.

'You are what you eat,' said Chetty Papa that day, and so the Gangwani Eighteen were baptized—named according to the produce on the estate for which they were responsible. Reminiscent of the true Seselwa socialist fashion in which Chetty Papa grew up on Mahé, this baptism was irrespective of nationality or religion. He didn't see Bangladesh, Sri Lanka, Nepal, Pakistan, or India in the company. From here on, they all had names of fruits they grew: Breadfruit, Passionfruit, Bilimbi, Mango, Frisiter (Golden Apple), and Red Lady. The rest were all named after local bananas: Kare, Miyonn, Misel, Papay, Gabou, Senzak, Mil, Fig, Rouz, Msye, Rezen, and Detab. The fruit names had given them a unique identity on the estate but they continued to be 'Malba' for the world outside. Chetty Papa called himself 'Lavocat', since he took personal interest and care in Avocados and their advocation and advertisement among the filthy rich folk of Eden Island. They were the most expensive produce of the estate.

As for Hitesbhai, a salt farmer had crossed the Indian Ocean to become a sweet fruit. He was the Red Lady of course—the Sunday fruit—which meant that while all other workers enjoyed their day off every weekend, he would still be working. Chetty Papa had given him a different schedule. For him, Wednesdays were off. Wednesdays were his Sundays for almost two years now—until the first Wednesday of that May.

III

EXPLANATION WAS NEVER a priority for the residents of Mahé. They did ask questions but were fine with any answer or none. They were assured of the fact that no matter where the road of curiosity takes them, they would end up home by sunset. Despite being surrounded by water from all sides for thousands of miles, thousands of residents did not know how to swim—they simply didn't feel the need to. For a country with just two highways—and both connected, it was a simple and satisfactory choice to make between the West Coast Road and the East Coast Road. They were sure of reaching their destination eventually and never getting lost. 'When in doubt, keep driving.' Moreover, the two coastal highways were further connected by two hill roads at several junctures in between—La Misere and Sans Souci—which provided the travellers with even more comfort, though these roads seemed deserted on holidays and came across as eerie to tourists who drove through the hills after dark.

'Why is it so creepy in the hills?' asked Hitesbhai after coming back from his first Sunday Delivery to the Waro House. 'Because of *greegree*,' Chetty Papa replied. It was the simplest ancient explanation that had been the standard response from every local to this 'outsider' question since forever. *Greegree* was a broad umbrella term which included black magic, voodoo, witchcraft, and other supernatural local occult rituals. Chetty Papa did not feel the need to explain further. Hitesbhai would keep discovering things that corroborated the practices of greegree on his subsequent Sunday Deliveries along with the estate's pick-up truck driver, Steve. They would take detours from the coastal highways onto the La Misere and Sans Souci roads to visit solitary viewpoints spread along the granite mountain ridge of Mahé that commanded the central landscape of the island. At these points they would occasionally find chalk-drawn pentagrams, shards of broken blue mirrors, nailed bananas, blood-stained iron needles, tall pebble mounds, and other mysterious stuff that Steve referred to as '*tanzani* things.'

'They are not Christians and they are not Creole! They come from outside and spread this here. Seychelles is not main Africa; we have moved far from these *tanzani* things. This was our past. The future is different. I spit on this, Red Lady!' Steve told Hitesbhai while standing in the middle of a huge pentagram beside the Rock Pool at Taka Maka, the southern-most district of Mahé. They were both surprised to find the remains of what seemed to be an elaborate occult ceremony. The same spot had been clean, undisturbed granite just a week back. Months later, both would think of this ominous find as an indicator of all the strange things that were to take place on the island in the coming days.

On his arrival, Hitesbhai could not really gauge what was normal or abnormal about Mahé, since this was the first time he had been out of his own country. It was Steve, his Sunday companion who revealed to Hites the quaint secrets of the island in broken English. Hites picked up those broken pieces with the limited English that he had learnt at the village school and put them together to form a dotted mind map of quaint unexplained happenings that characterized Mahé.

'It started with victory, Red Lady (referring to Hiteshbhai's given name),' he said on one of the early Sunday Deliveries. 'When people won the island back from old comrades two years ago, the old comrades ran to the Gulf. From there they cursed the people and sent back a virus to finish the island. And our victory turned into loss—of life and money for more than a year. The virus ended but the curse kept going even after that.' He added that several fires broke out around Victoria because of the comrades' curse and then showed Hites the charred remains of the top floor of Le Chantier Mall building. 'There used to be a disco here where they did *tanzani* stuff with fire and had to pay for it. Red Lady, if you worship the Devil, he will hug you with fire.' *That was not a convincing explanation*, Hitesbhai thought. But he had seen enough of the island by now to not care about explanations anymore. That was a fact. The entire circumference of Mahé was a little less than a two-hour drive, which meant Hitesbhai and Steve saw the whole island thrice every Sunday.

The Sunday Delivery had been institutionalized as a rather simple affair since the days of youth of Beny Waro—three Red Ladies and three raw mangoes were to be harvested at the Gangwani Estate, cut into fine pieces, and delivered to the Waro House by end of mass. He was particular about two Red Ladies being ripe for juice and fruit bowl and one Red Lady being raw—to be grated and sauteed for papaya salad. All mangoes were used for mango salad—a sweet and sour local delicacy made from the fusion of raw mangoes, lemons and onions. Hitesbhai undertook this Sunday Delivery in the pick-up truck driven by Steve who called it his weekly pilgrimage—for Beny Waro was kind of a God himself. Everyone claimed to believe in his existence but only a few had seen him. He had become a recluse since the comrades left the archipelago. Everything had changed since the old guard's exit. If there was an old guard left from the old guard it was Beny Waro. And the only thing that did not change for him was the Sunday Delivery.

Beny Waro was rich enough to be invisible. He wasn't like the chic bourgeois of Eden Island who stayed together in an expensive and exclusive commune of the elite with manicured beaches, lawns, and yacht decks; and whose bridge with the Mahé folk was literally a bridge with security kiosks on either end. Beny Waro was a proud Seselwa who believed that his country must be ruled by his own people and not outsiders—and so he went ahead to rule it himself, even though as distantly as possible. Ironically, he was in reality a 'resident outsider' just like everyone who lived on these islands that never had a native populace. He inherited majority of the islands in the archipelago from his father who disappeared on one of them never to return, and went on to consolidate his hold on these territorial jewels spread across the Indian Ocean. How did his father come to own all these islands? Explanation of this has never been sought by anyone reaffirming the blissful island spirit of ignorance.

Beny Waro realized very early that though a hundred thousand Seselwa lived on just fifteen islands of the one hundred and fifteen islands, the country was not only its people—it was also the hundred other islands with no human habitation. 'Do you know there are no wild animals on any of the islands of this country?' Chetty Papa said to Hitesbhai once. 'That's wrong. There is one. Right on top of that hill. Beny Waro!'

'And we must feed him every Sunday to keep him alive. To keep ourselves alive. The divine spirit must not go hungry,' added Steve loading his pick-up with the Sunday Delivery cart. 'Or there will be chaos!'

And there was chaos—with no explanation. The very next month after Hitesbhai's arrival, the monsoon had arrived too; rather aggressively. It ripped across the neighbouring islands of Praslin and La Digue destroying the jetties and embankments. Power systems failed temporarily and schools that had reopened just a week ago on Mahé were declared shut again. The National Day parade in June, which had been cancelled during the coronavirus pandemic, was postponed to July due to torrential rains.

'When will the parade happen, Minister?' a journalist had asked in the press conference.

The Minister had replied, 'Next Sunday.'

'Why Sunday, Minister? Would the storms stop and the monsoon leave by Sunday?'

The Minister had left without further explanation and everyone had seemed satisfied.

The chaos ensued—because the monsoon did leave by Sunday—never to return. A dry spell began on Mahé for three long months. All the little streams down the hills dried up and several reservoirs were left waterless. The height of Lagog dam was increased with the help of Beny Waro's expat workers, for whom his instructions were enough. When they asked for a hike in wages, he simply sent a message appreciating their efforts towards greater social good. The workers wondered more about their efforts since increasing the height of a dam with decreasing water levels did not convince them. They took up the matter with the only 'wild animal' in the country through the zookeepers of his house on the hill. They received a reply through the Sunday Delivery by Steve. Expats were asked to stop asking for explanations.

Chaos continued—because within a few hours of the Public Utility issuing drought warnings for the entire year, thunderstorms lashed Seychelles. The rain gods seemed so angry that the whole sowing season was devastated for most of the farming estates on the islands. The Gangwani Estate, being closest to the backwater channels near the ocean, remained flooded for weeks. The produce, however, was unaffected largely since all of them mostly dealt in fruits. But their living quarters were all filled with water. They sent a message over to the Waro House through Steve, requesting for a dry and safe temporary shelter somewhere higher up in the hills until the storms stopped. The Sunday after, Hitesbhai had gone with Steve to deliver the usual assortment of papayas and mangoes and to receive a response on the request.

'What did he say?' Hitesbhai asked Steve as he jumped back onto the driver seat.

'His housekeeping lady said flood relief is only for locals, not expats.'

To this, like a good expat masquerading as a local, Red Lady did not demand any explanation and they both quietly rolled downhill in the pick-up.

The year dragged on in submerged existence. Seasons stopped seasoning; fall was rainfall. The storms did not leave for months. They poured over the usually breezy October and soaked the usually hot November. Christmas came and so did the New Year, but what did not come was the sun. Thousands of white rich folks who had come to escape the dark wet winters of their Europe to enjoy 'the sun, the sand, and the sea' as claimed by Seychelles tourism ads in the newspapers and on instagram, were stuck indoors in their resort rooms using sunscreens as mere lubricant. All this while, the sun was there, the sand was there, and so was the sea, however, never together at the same time anywhere.

And then suddenly one day in March, the sun was back—bright and blazing. Within two days it desiccated the island—green palms shrunk into brown cripples and cinnamon crackled from within. A thick black cloud of smoke levitated like a cigarette puff from god's own mouth—an exhaled mass of black poisonous sins—including the massacre of eighty-four sea turtles in the outer islands by three soldiers of the state who smuggled that forbidden meat on the shipping stock at the break of newfound spring in March. 'Two days of sin has brought upon us a third day of excess and punishment,' the Religious Headmaster wrote on the Gossip Corner, as the country prepared itself to fight a huge fire in its biggest landfill that lay just beside the airport. As international flights made grand entries in and out of the black clouds of smoke to make brave landings on the concrete runway, fire brigades assembled next door to keep splashing water and red soil onto the flaming shite. It took tons of soil and tanks of water over three days to douse the fire that had singlehandedly shattered the Air Quality Index of the island—as pointed out by the Local Ecologist on the Gossip Corner. Even after the fire was over, she shared videos of melting polar caps on the same Facebook group as the unbearable heat continued.

The responses she received on these videos included heart emojis and 'Wish I was There' gifs.

In April, the fire department and the local police sat together over some breadfruit chips and decided to 'make hay while the sun (literally) shines' and investigate the landfill fire outbreak case to ascertain its causes. The investigation didn't reach any conclusion and no explanation was given—until the same landfill caught fire again in October that year. The explanation came from the Art-loving Politician who declared online, 'This is not smoke but black ash. It is not killing, but cleansing!' And so, everyone breathed in particulates for another three days.

Schools remained closed on the entire east coast of the island where the burning landfill stood adding red, orange, and black to the green and blue landscape of Mahé. Schools of the west coast felt terribly left out as they would have also liked an excuse to get a few holidays. Some children of the west coast felt bored of clean air, sweet breeze, and crystal-clear water so they started collecting sand from the west coast beaches in small plastic bags. They would then inhale dirt from these bags and lie on the beach for the entire day, bunking school. Their fathers went on fishing sorties and their mothers went to work in Victoria every day. They would come back by sunset and find the kids still chilling on the beach with their plastic bags of sand. They felt content about their children staying together in the neighbourhood and taking care of each other. This is how the heat was being beaten on the western flank of Mahé—no explanations sought—until the kids started falling sick. Some stopped eating, some puked their intestines out on the beach, and the others seem to have undergone irretrievable nervous breakdowns. The parents loaded all the children onto a neighbourhood pick-up truck and reached the only hospital on the island in Victoria. The Indian doctors could not be reached, the Cuban doctors could not be understood, the Chinese doctors could not be explained, and the Seselwa doctors could not be seen. It was a cleaning lady, on her way to dump a stock of spoilt bandages and syringes, who told the parents clearly, 'Ey Maman! Ey Papa! What your kids inhale from plastic bags is not sand.'

On receiving an unsolicited explanation from an unexpected source, the parents took some time to gauge the situation. The explanation was correct even though no one asked for it—those plastic bags were not full of beach sand, but cocaine. The kids were taken from the Victoria hospital to the Victoria police station. The lone inspector examined the plastic bags and within a microsecond declared, 'These are from Glacis district. Go to the Glacis police station.' The parents did not ask why. They nodded and the pick-up truck went straight to the police station in the Glacis district, a place in the north western part of Mahé, famous for its astute sea-faring fishermen. 'These plastic bags are from here. They are full of cocaine,' mamas and papas told the Glacis policeman who neither reverted to this complaint nor questioned the claim. He opened a register to register the case and penned down the entire story that the mamas and the papas dictated. He told them that the case will be forwarded to the CID and asked them to leave. In a minute, he realized that he had not taken down any names on the register, but the pick-up had left. He thought hard and convinced himself that he had seen one of the sand-inhaling boys a few months ago, playing football with 'David' printed on his jersey. He wrote the name 'David' at the top of the report in the register. Little did he know that the same register would disappear in a month, and the Glacis police station would be shut down forever due to repeated instances of paranormal activity.

The inexplicable series of events continued in the form of the Ghost of Glacis—a paranormal presence who would slap the policemen on night duty. Three similar slaps were reported after the 'David' report in the complaint register. All three cases were filed against the Ghost of Glacis. And when the fourth slap occurred one midnight, the policemen on duty abandoned the post—never to return. The permanent closure of the police station was announced a week later and there was no further demand for any explanation. The complaint records disappeared, the policemen stayed away from the station, the parents kept their children away from sandy plastic bags, and that is how all cases were solved. No pending action or explanation. Mahé was at peace.

The peace was broken in a few days by a political onslaught when the government charged the opposition of using witchcraft against its leaders. The police force that had now increased in strength after the closure of a station was deployed to investigate and arrest the accused. The island came in global spotlight for this quaint state of affairs that allegedly presented a unique method of dissent—black magic. A handful of locals were jailed along with a Tanzanian soothsayer and the controversy reached all corners. 'I tell you this *tanzani* stuff is no good, Red Lady!' said Steve angrily to Hitesbhai. 'They dug up graves in Taka Maka to put voodoo dolls of politicians. These are old dirty tricks. Like children. All of them collect sandy polyethene and get kicks from it to do this stuff.' Hitesbhai asked Steve what were voodoo dolls. On learning about them, he exclaimed that there was a similar practice in his village where potatoes were poked by sticks and carved into human-resembling statuettes to be put in fire with red chilies to ward off evil spirits. Steve was not surprised somehow. 'Yes, I'm sure. You Malba have that stuff. Snakes and old magicians and musical turbans. You all understand this *tanzani* stuff,' he said. Hitesbhai disapproved of the lack of surprise matter-of-fact judgmental tone of Steve's voice. It was also the first time that he sensed an element of disrespect in the term 'Malba' that had been an endearing title for him till now. He insisted on always being called 'Red Lady' thereafter.

The whole world looked at Seychelles with puzzled eyes. There were countless African countries in the eyes of the West which had had a fair share of coups—through political, military, and even insurrectional means—however, this was the first time that an alleged coup was being attempted through witchcraft. A four-month long stint of unexplained frenzy continued in the heart of Victoria and then all the charges were dropped by the court. But the world had stopped deriving its dopamine from this quaint outlandish voodoo headlines, until something extraordinarily crazy occurred on the seventh of December twenty-twenty-three on Mahé. The island witnessed unprecedented disaster that day.

What happened on seventh of December shook the Gangwani Eighteen to the core. Even Chetty Papa, who had always had deep gratitude for his boss Beny Waro, was left confused and scared. It was bigger than the case of the disappeared million dollars from the Gulf which the people had stopped discussing. It was bigger than the question of the ownership of Waro House that had been built on government land reserved for tropical biodiversity—supposedly bought for just one dollar by Beny's father. It was bigger than the unregulated activities that happened beyond the shores of Mahé, on the hundred odd islands that no common folk had ever been to. What happened on the seventh of December woke Hitesbhai up from the dream that he had been living in this paradise of a place. It exposed everything that was wrong with a community suffering from the absence of inquiry. It showed how vulnerable a perpetually stable isolated utopia could be in the face of accidental adversity.

In many ways, the seventh of December was a prologue to first of May. The former was the first instance that the men at Gangwani finally started asking questions. And the first of May was when they received an explanation—in the form of premature reddening of the Red Ladies—and how time was warping: turning Wednesdays into Sundays, and Hitesbhai into a hero.

IV

ON THE SEVENTH of December, a state of emergency was declared in the Republic of Seychelles. That day, the entire island of Mahé had woken up three hours before the crack of dawn. It was a crack nonetheless that had woken them up—a supersonic crack. For the people of the west coast, it felt like a cloudburst. Since they were facing torrential rains for about a week already, it felt like a thunderclap that had gushed a cloud straight down the hills and onto the beaches. For the people of the east coast who were on the so-called 'leeward side' of the granite mountains, the crack was much more of a boom originating from the industrial area of Providence district. The people were tossed from their beds in the darkness of confusion. A reverberating blast had shattered the glass of all buildings around the Providence area and had even pushed open the bolted windows, doors, and ventilators of buildings… up till Victoria. People ran out of their homes terrorized; they were on the streets trying to find out what had happened. They needed an explanation at this highly inconvenient hour. They gathered around each other and recorded the destruction of their houses and posted it on the Gossip Corner. All they could do apart from that, was wait till eight in the morning when the authorities would dispatch two cavalcades of fire brigade and ambulance units from Victoria—one to the east coast and the other to the west. The west coast team would discover a collapsed home with three residents buried in flooded debris, while the east coast team would witness absolute pandemonium in Providence—where an industrial grade blast had occurred at the local factory of explosives.

Hitesbhai's dreams were usually quiet and boring—sometimes he would find himself playing hide and seek in the salt mounds at the outskirts of his village, other times he would be throwing stones in the sky and catching them back. A few odd nights were more anxious, when he would find himself drowning in the ocean with no one around for miles. Or when he would be driving Steve's pick-up truck off a cliff, or sometimes, when he would be squeezing the breasts of Beny Waro's housekeeping lady, who would also spread her ebony legs at the gate of Waro House for Hitesbhai in his dream. He would be basking in the glory of his lost virginity and wake up suddenly to wrap and squeeze his soiled pyjamas. Such nights were inconvenient for the body, but reassuring for the soul—even on an island far away, Hites felt as much alive and fulfilled in dreams as he would be anywhere else. The night that announced the arrival of seventh December was no such night.

Everyone was deaf. That was the first thing Hitesbhai registered in his visibly shaken constitution. The Gangwani Eighteen were already on the road before they realized they had woken up from their beds and had run across the estate to escape the sound of catastrophe. The supersonic crack had censored their ears to the sound of a shrilling beep that vibrated their bodies all at once. Some thought it was a tsunami siren. Some thought it was a terrorist attack. Others were still asleep with eyes open and ears deaf—they perhaps thought that they were already dead. Within minutes, the east coast road was flooded with expat workers from the neighborhood: construction workers, farm workers, factory laborers, office attendants, and menial workmen who had run away from their dormitories and camps to find out which alien invasion had occurred past midnight.

This was the first time Hitesbhai saw how huge the expat community was on the island. A large populace of South Asian men, segregated in different company compounds limiting their access from each other and the world beyond, were out in the open this night—reaching out to each other's injured bodies. Hitesbhai felt like a stranger who had found his own folk finally, though in unfortunate circumstances. Beneath the shrill in his eardrum, he heard men shouting in Gujarati, his mother tongue. He made an effort to mumble something, but this was not the time for greeting. Hazy sights whizzed past him as his eyes recoiled: a burnt face, a broken hand, a paralyzed leg, a ripped chest, some fainted beings lying on the pavement.

A fire blazed across the road—with nothing around it. The blast had struck everything down to rubble. Trees annihilated. It felt like a forest had been erased from the periphery of the east coast road—the curtain of the ancient tropical canopy had been burnt down and now what remained of it was naked nothingness built from shattered glass and debris. A group of workers stormed the pharmacy on the highway that had been disemboweled by the impact. They snatched medicines and bandages and ran out towards the casualties. They knew about first-aid well, since two of them worked at the same pharmacy themselves. They knew they would be losing their jobs after this incident—in a way it made them happy—knowing the end of their contract was near and this was an opportunity to help brothers in need. It would be a heroes' farewell eventually.

The crumbling and crunching of glass shards continued in the background of a chaotic war effort in the street. Brothers carrying brothers in arms, collecting the injured at the bus stop shed waiting for the ambulance. Heavy breathing, crying and beating of concrete prevailed causing an overarching dizziness in the mind of Hitesbhai who suddenly thought that the only person who could make sense of the situation was Chetty Papa! However, he was nowhere to be seen. The Gangwani men had gathered together and all fruits seemed to be present next to the bus shed—except the Avocado. Hites ran back.

Faint screams in his mother tongue tried to stop Hitesbhai from running in the opposite direction to search for Chetty Papa. His brain seemed to have split into two—one that looked back and deciphered these Gujarati calls of caution emanating a strange sense of familiarity in the face of travesty and the other pushed him forward in the scrounge for Chetty Papa—the one who had been his real family on the island, despite being an alien who spoke a different tongue and knew nothing about his home. One part of his conscience belonged to 'Hitesbhai' and the other to the 'Red Lady'!

He jumped over the wall and pushed aside the flimsy fence of the Gangwani Estate running across the rows of banana trees and straight towards the dormitory entrance which looked like a bombed bunker next to war trenches.

The doors and windows had been ripped out of the cuboidal concrete that was the sleeping shelter to eighteen men just a few minutes ago. Hitesbhai cried out, 'Papa! Chetty Papa!' slowly making way through the haze in the room. He called out a few more times, and then noticed some movement in the debris near an arched corner that had been a kitchen a few minutes ago. A big slab of granite moved aside to reveal a middle-aged man with torn clothes pricked by glass shards across the torso. It was Chetty Papa puffing dust, bleeding profusely and holding two avocados in his hands. He would be taken to the hospital in a few hours where he would hand over the two avocados to Hitesbhai saying, 'I looked for precious things in the room before running out. This was all we had, it seems.'

Chetty Papa would be treated and discharged the next day. Hitesbhai would be in the waiting room of the hospital watching the local TV news announcing that the seventh December disasters had claimed three lives due to the torrential rains, however, no one died in the factory blast. Hundreds had been injured yet there were no deaths—not even the guards or the workers living in the factory. Gangwani men discussed how there had been no one on duty inside or around the location that night. Something seemed terribly fishy, but no one expected any explanation from the authorities. The state of emergency was repealed within twelve hours and the President ordered a probe into the causes of the blast. A year would pass in criminal investigation with no conclusion as expected, but the memory of that night would be etched in the minds of the people—who would eventually rebuild their homes, their workplaces and their lives—knowing nothing about the person who changed it that fateful night.

Even though there were no lives lost in the blast, one man came close to dying from his injuries. A man who was left alone in the emergency ward starving for blood—noticed by Hitesbhai while getting off the ambulance with a bleeding Chetty Papa; a man from the past whose apathy had returned in a deadly form to haunt him—and perhaps bleed him to death. A man who had bled the salt farms of his hometown and along with that the salt farmers who depended on it for their lives. A man who wasn't supposed to be anywhere around the Indian Ocean, but in an almost completely opposite place on the globe: America! It was Hittalbhai Pandya—unconscious, helpless, almost dead red on the stretcher. Red Lady looked him right through the oxygen mask and murmured something he hadn't for a long while since leaving home: '*bainchod*!'

2

THE SHARK

V

THE PLAN WAS simple. And it was as clear cut as the cubes of the dead shark kept at the back of Steve's pick-up truck to dry in the sun. Hitesbhai informed Steve that a Sunday Delivery had to be done despite it being a Wednesday on the first of May. The Red Ladies had spoken, he said. He needed to take them to Waro House and then discuss the next contract for all the Gangwani men before they were shipped to Esomption Estate by weekend, with Beny Waro. Steve was sorting the shark cubes and broke into laughter hearing the name of Beny Waro.

'No one has seen God before, Red Lady! Beny Waro is unreachable.'

'Not today. It is the first of May.'

Steve acknowledged. It was time for the Labor Day brunch for Beny Waro. For his annual special '*Satini Reken'*—the creole Shark *Chutney*! The housekeeping lady at the Waro House would be waiting for a kilogram of dried tiger shark cubes. 'And some delicious papayas can be great for starters,' Hitesbhai remarked as he put a bag of three ripe Red Ladies on to the front seat of the truck.

Steve realized they had little time. They had to reach on top of the hill within an hour. He rushed to get a fistful of salt, shouted 'Reken!' and threw the salt onto the shark cubes.

'Let's go!'

The pick-up consisting of three papayas, two men, and one kilogram of tiger shark whizzed off the Gangwani Estate as its residents looked on in the hope of a renewed pact with their 'God.' Hites carried their produce and their voice up the hill.

Reken was not just an ordinary tiger shark. It was not only a few kilograms of cubes sold across Mahé on the first of May, but also a few kilolitres of saltwater trapped in its skeletal cage while being soaked in a pool of melting ice inside big blue plastic containers with thermocol seals onboard the boat that brought it to the shore of the island. It was more as a whole than the sum of its parts—that now lay distributed and digested in Seselwa bellies.

Reken had lived a short, but honorable life as an adult shark. She had been a respectable—feared rather than loved—but nonetheless respected figure among the marine colonies of the south western Indian Ocean. A dominating disposition. An intimidating presence. A swift personality. A lethal existence. A quintessential tiger shark—before being very much dead on the eve of Labor Day that year.

If an obituary were to be crafted for poor old scary dear Reken, it would have been something on the lines of 'Missing: The Ghost of Saint Helena.' She was, in fact, the Ghost of Saint Helena for over a couple of years now. She was already dead for thousands of fish, turtles, crustaceans, dolphins, and millions of planktons who lived and survived Reken and her kin in the Atlantic waters between the coasts of Saint Helena Island and West Africa. These waters were home and hunting grounds at the same time for a flourishing blood-thirsty marine community dominated by the ancestors of Reken for centuries until a deadlier force invaded.

The community along Saint Helena had thrived on the simple principle of 'big fish eat small fish' for millions of years under water until the small fish realized that there were bigger fish above water.

'Fish that walked on water and flew in the sky,' gargled the sea turtles who would get a sneak peek now and then on the surface. The dolphins confirmed this. And that struck fear in them. 'We would prefer being eaten by the sharks,' remarked the squid squad, 'than these devils from the sky.' 'The devil you know is better than the devil you don't,' added the crayfish. The crabs informed that they had seen the bigger fish up close and that they did not look like fish at all. 'Even you don't look like fish but that isn't scary. You are still one of the first to be eaten,' said the lobsters. The octopuses inked at the irony.

There were stories of how huge steel boards appeared on the surface and suddenly dropped cages and chambers pulling massive nets across the reef. And in this setting of confusion and fear everyone swam for cover: the turtles, the dolphins, the crustaceans, and all that breathed—under the rocks, beneath the corals and along the seabed. However, the one lone grumpy tiger made way through the silent waters, baring its frightening canines and pumping grim bubbles of aggression: its fins smooth yet sharp, its tail swift yet charming, its beak lethal yet graceful, its eyes terrifying yet determined.

Tiger sharks are a majestic, illusive, and overpowering breed just like tigers. They have tiger stripes streamlined along their lower bodies. These stripes disappear with age and an average adult with a decent diet may grow into the size of a minivan. Reken was the size of Steve's pick-up truck before she was chopped into pieces. But what made Reken special was not what she did with the 'bigger fish' that came parked on the surface on their giant steel boards, it was her journey from being a predator to being a prey. And it was a story that the crustaceans whispered among themselves as the lore of the Ghost of Saint Helena—a terror that was eventually terrorized by something greater, something incomprehensible from below, something invincibly deadly from above.

Before the first steel boards arrived, the Helena reef was ruled by the orcas. They were the biggest baddest boys in the area—inspiring fear and awe in the lives of other denizens across the southern Atlantic. Every dignified living swimming creature wondered if the orcas were whales or dolphins. Some dolphins proudly claimed orcas to be dolphins until they saw them eat other dolphins. And whales didn't really claim anything, they moved in massive packs and the orcas feasted on them as well. Basically, you needed to be scared of orcas because you might be eaten by them, irrespective of your identity—whether it be shark, dolphin, ray, fish, sea mammals, or even a sailboat floating on rough seas.

'Beny Waro is an orca,' Steve declared and giggled.

This interrupted the train of thought on which Hitesbhai was traveling as the pick-up moved across Victoria and onto the mountain road of Sans Souci. He had been thinking deeply about what to say to Beny Waro, how to confront him, and how to clearly put forward the demands of the farm workers. He was making a mental brief of the demands. One: medical cover and insurance. Two: dry and safe shelter. Three: monthly mobile internet package. Four: holiday on Sundays. Five: ban on the use of the term 'Malba' for expats. These were demands from not just an angry Indian laborer but from the alienated Gangwani eighteen. And Chetty Papa had concurred. These were fair demands to be considered for the next contract before the team got shipped to Esomption Estate for the construction of a Waro resort there. Waro resorts were being planned on several islands of the country and the burden of their construction was upon the faithful hardworking expat South Asian labor who were apparently ready to work for a ridiculously cheap wage with no added safety assurances. What if they get eaten up by a shark on the way? That was Hitesbhai's worry. A shark was the epitome of marine fear for him. He still didn't know what orcas were.

'Orca?' He looked at Steve puzzled.

'Killer whale.'

'But Beny Waro is a shark. Wild animal!'

'A shark's nothing, Red Lady! There's one kept chopped behind us.'

'But shark is most dangerous.'

'Orcas eat sharks for breakfast, Red Lady! Literally!'

'I have never seen an orca.'

'Well, nor have I! I don't know anyone here who has seen an orca. But everyone knows they are around somewhere. Which is why Beny Waro is more of an orca than a shark. Invisible and powerful.'

'But his house lady from Kenya sees him.'

'Well, you never know. Many people believe that I see him every week too. But that is not true. I can never get past the gate.'

'Have you ever asked to go meet him?'

Steve looked irritated at this.

'Would you ever want to ask to meet an orca, Red Lady? And that too without any reason? Just to say hello?'

Hitesbhai did not answer. He thought about the tiger shark cubes and the salt sprinkled on them. The same salt that he and his parents worked so hard to make—only to be wasted in this case on a dead fish being brought for a bigger fish to eat.

Like Hites, Reken too came from a salty background. She came from the warm salty latitudes of south western Atlantic which were once perfect for breeding and feeding. However, things evolved in strange incomprehensible ways for all denizens of Reken's home—just as for the salt farmers of Kutch. The equator was like the mirror parting for Hitesbhai's Gujarat and Reken's Saint Helena. Their original homes lay on the opposite sides of sub-Saharan Africa along two different oceans. But today they were the passengers of the same truck—in whole, and in parts, alive and dead.

The salt on the shark cubes reminded Hitesbhai of his encounter with Hittalbhai on the fateful day of the disaster of seventh December. A lot had changed in the six months since that meeting. He did not hold any grudges against Hittalbhai anymore. Seeing the horrendous situation in which Hittalbhai lay oozing blood at the Victoria hospital, Hites volunteered to donate blood to save his old landlord's life. He gained a lot that day just by losing a few milliliters of blood. He did not only feel redeemed but rewarded after talking to Hittalbhai, but that was a memory to be thought of later—Hites focused on the road again.

'If Beny Waro is an orca… Who is the shark?' he asked Steve.

'You are, Red Lady! Get ready to be chopped and distributed.'

They laughed and the truck rolled on.

Steve was correct in a lot of ways. Reken and Hites moved away from home to seek a better home for themselves. Homes that unfortunately fell short of accepting them. Homes that put them in further danger. Years ago, when the wind and the sun began changing ways for the whole Helena reef, orcas were the first to flee the zone. They were big and powerful and could move greater distances towards the ice caps down south. That left Reken and her family on top of the power pyramid. And a few years of shark domination ensued. The visits by steel boards also increased: massive fishery vessels, oil containers, patrolling boats, fishing trawlers and what not! The life underwater could only make myths and folk tales out of what they were witnessing on the canvas of water and sunlight from the seabed. The ecosystem knew that the sharks were deadly, but there were even deadlier entities above the reef.

Reken's childhood was healthy. She faced some teething issues but more or less, she lived up to her terrifying antecedents. She was a scary shark for the local marine populace and having never seen an orca or any other apex predator in her home waters, she had a decently safe adolescence. As she began outgrowing her tiger scales while transforming into an adult lone hunter who would spread fear more effectively, she began noticing changes in the sun and the wind as hinted by her elders. Sharks never listened to their elders—that was never a part of their etiquette or lifestyle. In fact, they could afford to be dismissive to the elders' teachings since they were anyway always alert and always awake. The two sides of their brains never let them sleep and were always proactive in sensing any kind of suspicious activity, whether it be inches apart or miles away.

Reken could sense it all: oil, sewage, ink, and blood—mixing in the depths of the waters across which she ruled. She had become familiar to these alien releases from the steel boards. These alien elements seemed to interfere with her ability to navigate the reef. And with time, the salts became deceiving—the less salty areas got saltier, and the saltier areas seemed to have lost their salt. Reken found it harder and harder to move and hunt. Moreover, her catch was being snatched from her by the alien boards from above. Her 'territory,' that had been acquired from the orcas, appeared to be drifting away to the foreigners who could change the wind and the sun as they pleased.

Reken starved for days sometimes, in search of adequate meals. The whole colony seemed to be subject to massive trawling. Unimaginably big invasive nets dropped from the steel boards before the sun came out—and in the dark early hours of the day a whole marine city would be uprooted and kidnapped—never to be seen again by Reken and her kin. The tiger sharks did their best to adapt by expanding their dietary options—discarded tins of meat, bottle caps, plastic bags, slime, waste, and whatever solid garbage the steel boards were kind enough to part with. These caused grave digestive problems to Reken initially, however, in a few years' time she had developed an appetite for everything novel. In some time, she looked forward to getting a taste of spoilt red meat, expired bacon strips, smelly chicken wings, and a particularly rancid portion of lamb cuttings. But with this assorted land mammal cuisine, came the absolutely catastrophic experience of biting through toxic stickers, plastic coatings, occasional metal bolts, and glass shards. These ripped apart the insides of many tiger sharks. Some were immobilized, others rendered emaciated.

Reken survived these days of oceanic famine in the reef gracefully. She was the most ambitious of her lot—a lone lethal hunter who was ready to go to any extreme in search of a delicious big loggerhead turtle or a crispy leatherback. On certain dusks, when the moon was just right, she ventured along the coast of Saint Helena to catch one of these turtles unaware. Reken loved sea turtles. Digging her pretty canines into the flippers and tearing them apart from the shell—the whole process of scooping out some exquisite flesh from an inverted sealed bowl was enjoyable for her. It was like eating oysters underwater for tiger sharks.

'If I am shark. Who is my prey?' asked Hitesbhai.

'A shark eats whatever it wants, Red Lady. So, whatever you find is your food,' replied Steve. Hitesbhai thought about his diet. He thought how the food for the Gangwani men depended on monthly import shipments. There were a few months when there was no flour available on the island, which meant no Indian bread—no *puris*, no *chapatis*, no *parathas*. Hitesbhai ate rice every day with the watery dal prepared by Chetty Papa. The other estate workers were fine chewing on chicken and mutton and beef and pork, but for Hitesbhai even caramelized onions and garlic were gluttony. He was always careful to not talk about any of his dietary changes when on the weekly videocall with his family. He didn't want to unnecessarily create trouble exposing his sins.

'You are what you eat,' he would repeat to Chetty Papa, 'and I am clean!'

The weekly videocall was special for Hites. He got a chance to see the pixelated faces of his family back home. On festivals, his mother would make some sweet treats and show him. It would make his mouth water. This would tempt him to spare some change and go to the Gopi sweet shop just across the road from the estate compound. He would buy half a kilogram of *jalebis* for himself—crispy, red, and juicy. *Jalebis were like the papayas of oil and sugar,* he thought. 'They are basically unhealthy Red Ladies,' Chetty Papa concurred. Gopi was the only Indian sweet shop in the country. It ran a decent business of international trade and local catering before being almost completely destroyed by the seventh December disaster. The business had to be rationalized after that and therefore, the catering had to stop. This broke Hitesbhai's heart. His sweet tooth needed other remedies.

'An island in this ocean eats to grow,' continued Steve, 'and that can mean the end of many things. Like the crocodiles or the dodos or the millions of bats we caught and ate.' Hitesbhai knew about the fruit bats—they were a local delicacy—and dodos didn't ring any bells. However, the moment he heard Steve say 'crocodiles' he was visibly startled. 'Dodos were all over from Mauritius, Red Lady! We could never see one... but the island ate them up. And I am sure that is what is going to happen to all the animals in Comoros and Madagascar too. The islands will eat them up.'

'No. Crocodiles!' Hites remarked.

'Yes, crocodiles. They were all over Seychelles for centuries.'

'Then what...'

'The French came and ate them all.'

'When?'

'Well, it took them a hundred years to finish all of them. They came here to rule before the British did the same.'

'Oh! The British did same with us,' Hitesbhai seemed to understanding this now.

'They ate all your crocodiles?'

'No no. They ruled us for hundreds of years.'

'But they left your crocodiles alone. So that's mighty kind of them.'

Hitesbhai nodded but thought how it would have been so much better if all those *gharials* in his local saltwater streams back home were killed off by the British. He could have learned to swim that way—with no fear of being eaten by crocodiles.

'We are all sharks, Red Lady!' Steve declared, 'with salty sweaty skins waiting to be ripped.'

As the pick-up made its way through the mountain forest road, Steve and Hites peered at the dense sun-filtered canopy above their heads. Tourists with shorts and shoes on walked in tiny slim queues on the sides. They were overcautious about the vehicles on the road. Even on a single-lane highway, occasional blue bulky public buses drove past them at high speeds. The flowing rainwater streams on one edge and the dangerous road on the other made these tourist queues walk very slowly towards their destinations: they were heading towards the several trek routes on the road separated by just a couple of kilometres from each other—Morne Blanc, Salazie Trail, Morne Seychellois, Trois Freres peak, and others. Steve had done all of these trails as a young boy. 'When there were no buses and no taxis we walked all the way from our homes to all these peaks,' he had told Hites, 'and on the way we had to watch out for the gree-gree and the *tanzani* stuffs.'

The mountain of Trois Freres had a cross on its peak and on its way, there were numerous stories of people getting lost because of evil spirits and misguiding ghosts. It was normal to see voodoo rituals and some kind of occult ceremonies being performed along bonfires on the trail at night. 'But that was long ago,' Steve said, 'when everyone started going to church things got better. The hurt and lost spirits were healed by the lord.' *It was true*, Hites thought, as their truck passed the Trois Freres signboard, he had himself witnessed catholic congregations doing forest mass on the same trail every first Sunday of the month. He felt safe thinking that these eerie surroundings were being divinely sanitized every now and then.

The shady rituals of the supernatural, however, did continue in the hilly districts of Mahé as both of them discovered during their Sunday deliveries. Shark and turtle meats were being cooked in elaborate midnight feasts in the jungle. Shark meat was considered to be a source of magical powers—from enhanced sexual prowess to the ability of jumping high enough to catch a fruit bat. But all of these things were distant when seen from the other prominent areas of the island, say Victoria, the vibrant capital or Perseverance, the urban centre or Eden Plaza, the elite colony or even Providence, the commercial hub district. Common folk went about their lives comfortably ignoring all these activities that Steve couldn't stop calling '*tanzani* stuffs.' It was disconcerting for Hitesbhai to think this way of this island where he had been living for two years: a quaint *jalebi* of a place with twisted minds and confusing ways.

Reken did lose her family to human obsession for enhanced sexual prowess though. Shark meat was a hot commodity in the southern Atlantic. From small fishing boats to armadas of commercial fisheries—the intrusion of floating steel boards got bigger and scarier. Shark fins were a delicacy in the East and shark cartilage was an important ingredient in Chinese medicine which claimed to cure infertility, erectile dysfunction and premature ejaculation. This demand made fishing and finning rampant. Local activists complained of poaching and trawling, international activists considered it 'illegal, unreported, and unregulated' and everyone else called it 'business.' It was in fact, livelihood for the small fishermen and contractors hired by big fishing conglomerates.

From the islands of Seychelles too, thousands of men went on month-long fishing trips in high seas during the season. It was the only purely 'masculine' profession of the country. 'The country is run by Mamas, Red Lady!' Steve would say, 'Papas just fish and get drunk.' Women went to offices; men went to the sea. And from the sea, they brought with them some decent leftovers. Leftovers of the ocean—what the big European industrial giants left for the small local catchmen—all the tuna, shark, shrimp, and crab that escaped their nets destined for packaging and processing assembly lines in other continents found their way back to small motor boats that returned to Mahé. They would then be chopped and sold in the local fish markets. And along with the sea meats, a shipment of plastic packages containing cocaine and heroin would also arrive in the market. It would be *laissez-faire* for both—the big fisheries who took home the big catch, and the small fishermen who took home many small big catches!

Shark meat was also ideal for smuggling cocaine locally. Selling pounds of it sewed with plastic rendered it feasible for easy delivery to areas around Les Mamelles which were more inland and did not have a fish market of their own. These areas witnessed periodic explosions of young drug addicts depending on the seasonal flow of shipment. Drugs became more or less like any other commodity: rice, wheat flour, or vegetables. Further, shark meat also catered to customers hooked to something stronger: organized religion. Seafood was *halal* and that certification built a market of its own. Shark meat was a suitable replacement for red meat for many who were embracing Islam on the small island. Many locals were happy to look pious and go to the Victoria Mosque in exchange for some monetary and social benefit. The newly growing religious community did not place strict dietary restrictions; however, it was publicly appreciated if only kosher meat could be consumed. This left shark and tuna as favourites for steak.

Reken had little or no idea about how integral she was to the natural, social, and geo-political landscape of the steel boards and their people. Their lives were intertwined like the fishing nets that strangled her kith and kin. Hitesbhai now thought of the shark cubes kept at the back as a jigsaw puzzle. He wondered if he could collect and put all the cubes in order: will that re-assembled shark be the same as the tiger shark before being sliced? How much of it would be tiger and how much shark? Or would it never be the same without the plastic that lined its insides? It was a thought meandering towards the ship of Theseus. Alas, Hites knew nothing about Theseus or any ship. All he knew was that he was on Steve's four-tyred ship hoping to encounter an orca on top of the hill!

VI

HITTALBHAI PANDYA COULD never make it to America. Instead, he lay on a squeaky bed in Victoria Hospital trying to gather strength to bend his neck to see his ripped chest and broken ribs. His eyes were tired of staring at the ceiling whose cracks he had been observing for three weeks now. He thought of himself as a doctor to the ceiling—examining the cracks each day and praying for them to vanish. This was just like the hospital doctors who visited Hittalbhai each day and hoped for his torso, ribs and abdomen to repair themselves. The ceiling was a mirror. Every morning Hittalbhai woke up to see the same lines running from everywhere to everywhere. The dilapidated plaster and the shoddy cement patchwork seemed to show him how his body had been stitched together after being blown to smithereens on seventh December. If it were not for a known stranger's help, he could not have made it.

The known stranger sat next to him to welcome the new year as both their eyes traced some new cracks on the old ceiling. Hitesbhai had saved Hittalbhai from the clutches of death by donating his blood. After two weeks of recovery, Hittalbhai was told by the doctors about the stranger who had been there for him in this time of need. None of his colleagues, friends, or family had come to visit him, but this one blood donor named 'Hites' paid a visit twice a week but only to ask the doctors how the patient was. He never asked to meet him until New Year's Eve. Hittalbhai felt uneasy on knowing this. Sleep did not come easily that night—not that it had come easily lately, however, a mixture of gratitude, shame, and helplessness rode his mind in dark directions. He stopped the nurse from switching the lights off that night—he said he wanted to watch the ceiling.

Sleep did come—without him realizing. In the morning, he was surprised to see Hites beside the bed from the corner of his right eye. His left eye was still fixated at the ceiling. His heartbeat shot up. His jaw began trembling.

'You don't need to worry. I am just here for the report,' Hitesbhai said in Kutchi language. He was seated comfortably on a stool with a notepad in his lap on which he feigned scribbling notes as he looked towards the patient to respond.

'What report?' Hittalbhai asked in the language of their hometown. A mass of air heavy with history and familiarity creeped into the hospital room with the two men who knew so much about each other's past but so less about their present.

'I work as a news reporter,' lied Hitesbhai, 'I am covering the investigation of the seventh December blast.'

'I have lost a lot of blood, but not my mind. A Kutchi reporter in Seychelles? Tell that to someone else. I know you work for Waro at Gangwani.'

'How do you know that?'

'I have always known that. I know most of the expats here. I saw you at the embassy tree plantation drive last year,' he paused to breathe, the chest wounds were hurting, 'in fact

I told the agent to get you here from the salt farm. I wanted to make amends.'

Hitesbhai was taken aback. Before he could respond, Hittalbhai told him that he had failed to get an American visa even after selling the farm. All the money invested in preparing his file went down the drain because of a fake certificate. He and his family had come down to Mumbai for the visa appointment and the rejection of their application was almost immediate. The agent had failed to produce a good copy and the embassy officials were quick to detect the forgery. They were all stuck in Mumbai.

'Why didn't you come back to the farm?'

'There was no farm anymore. How could we come back to a whole village laughing at us? How could I come back to working with you people. I was the boss. It was my farm. It was my salt. You will never understand the humiliation. You know nothing.'

'But you could come back and build something bett…'

'Build what?! In the middle of nowhere! In a desert of salt which could give no one nothing!' he paused for breath and coughed three times before continuing, 'Your parents knew it. Everyone knows it. There was nothing left there. The Goddess is angry with us. For five years we had no profits. The unseasonal rains swept away hordes of my salt. Mountains of my salt were demolished by winds coming from nowhere! There can only be a curse behind it. The storms came every summer for five years continuously. That had never happened before. All our things, solar pumps, motors, rester, everything broke down because of the anger of the Goddess. We struggled to get any production. Everything was golden and useless. Nothing white. No salt. Just sand. You will not know. You are young. You know nothing. We had to run away! All your people have to run away!'

'And your family?'

'They are in Mumbai. I have debts to pay. All our savings were gone long back in trying to maintain the farm. And now medical bills will make things worse after this,' he shrugged at his immobile torso as his voice quivered, 'I will go back for treatment. The doctors say I cannot get better here. And like every other Malba, my expenses are not covered here. But thank you for everything, for the blood and…'

'I was just paying back for the salt, I guess,' Hites smirked.

'What do I owe you?'

'Just the truth.'

'About?'

'Why did no one come to help you? None of your coworkers turned up. None of the labor of your company came to help you. I asked around but no one was ready to talk about you. All I could gather was that you are a junior manager with Sakthi Builders. I am sure you treat the workers at the company like you treated my parents at the salt farm. By realizing that, I could understand why no one wanted to help you survive. Everyone wanted you dead.'

'Really? You think so? Then why did you save me?'

'Humanity.'

'You really think I am as naïve as you. No Malba comes to show humanity to other Malba here. And his life is as important to the Seselwa as a beer bottle cap. You helped me because you could feel powerful when you did so. And I can understand that feeling—of being in control, of being superior. By saving me you could show me who I had been and how terribly wrong I have been in all my decisions—that you didn't even know of. Did your parents ever say something bad about me? Did you ever see for yourself how I treated them?'

'You took away their daily bread without even…'

'I gave them their daily bread in the first place.'

'That does not change the truth.'

'Do you like it here?'

'Why do you …'

'Answer me.'

'Yes. It's better here.'

'Why is it better here?'

'I have a place to stay. I get a salary that is deposited every month in my parents' bank account at home. All the food, water, and electricity expenses are taken care of. And the work is not much. The people I live with are good people.'

'I told the same thing to the agent who brought you here.'

Hites fell silent.

'You like it because there is some dignity here. That is why I came here too. After being stuck in Mumbai, I was ready to lose all my money but I was not ready to face the disrespect that awaited me in the village. I could not return at any cost. The agent suggested going to Seychelles since it did not require any visa. I gave it a shot. And I liked it as much as you in the beginning. I was ready to do any dirty work in the company of strangers. The work I would never do back home.'

'Then your coworkers must like you. Why did they not come to check on you here?'

'Because they were not allowed to,' Hittalbhai's eyes welled up, 'Dignity is nothing without freedom. And your ignorance can only take you so far in shielding you from that. Once you start demanding freedom, your bread-givers will come together to push you down. And they will not let others follow your cause. I was quickly promoted to junior manager because of the good work I had been doing at the company, and that exposed me to many unsettling things. And I wanted to change things.'

At this point Hitesbhai felt the need to actually use the notepad he had in his hands. As Hittalbhai elaborated on his experience as a junior manager, Hites began taking down notes. He spoke about how brown labor was being exploited by brown bosses. Malba was flying in Malba from the subcontinent forcing all Malba to work for extended periods of time on a reduced wage. 'You may feel happy about your salary being given to your family back home every month. But it is much less than the fair share … what you could get in hand here if you were not Malba.'

But demanding fair wage could seem as being directly out of line, so the focus for dignity and freedom was an indirect meandering journey like a pick-up truck moving uphill. On the notepad, Hites had written four demands which Hittalbhai had begun asking for from his superiors: Safety, Accommodation, Connection, and Holiday. Hittalbhai, from his decent knowledge of domestic politics, had coined an acronym out of it: '*S.A.C.H.!*' which meant 'truth' in Hindi. He wrote of it in letters to the company administration and the human resource department. He also asked his coworkers to raise S.A.C.H. as a slogan. Hites listened and noted further: 'Safety' referred to security and medical insurance; 'Accommodation' meant having a suitable living space; 'Connection' was basically getting mobile subscription; and 'Holiday' implied the demand for getting Sundays and public holidays as rightful days-off.

'These were basic demands that I could see expats being refused,' Hittalbhai continued, 'while the local labor enjoyed all such entitlements. And as junior manager, I was asked to keep this discriminated approach going in the interests of the company.'

'But you decided to raise the issue?'

'Yes. And they took disciplinary action against me and kept me back on probation last month. I guess this blast is a blessing in disguise that way. It will forcefully send me back for medical reasons now. That is a dignified return. It is less humiliating than being fired. At least my wife and children can see how physically hard it has been for me.'

'Why do you say that?'

'Yes. Because that is what everyone thinks of this place. A pristine paradise with white tourists landing in their private jets to splurge dollars and euros on expensive trips in the middle of the ocean. My family is struggling badly in Mumbai and they think I am enjoying here. But I have none of the four things I wanted every worker to have here—to have a home away from home. The most beautiful places can be a step away from sudden collapse. Like this roof above my head right now.'

Suddenly a lull prevailed. Hites stared at the stitches and bandages adorning the frozen body of the patient while Hittalbhai got back to observing the cracks on the ceiling.

Steve suddenly honked twice at the approaching truck which disturbed Hitesbhai's recollection of his hospital visit to meet Hittalbhai five months ago. Honking twice was part of the prevalent vehicle lingo on the island: honking once was 'thank you', honking twice meant 'hello' and using the dipper meant 'after you.' Steve shouted '*Bonzour*' and waved at the passing truck. It was a big Ashok Leyland carrier with a whole regiment of Indian workers stacked in four rows like a herd of sheep. They looked messy, haggard, and happy. Some of them were chatting meekly, some were smiling across rows at each other while some were enjoying the breeze at the back. Someone from them screamed at Hitesbhai, 'All the best for Waro!' It seemed to him that some still knew about the four demands and the plan to propose the changes to the contract. Five months since Hittalbhai's departure had been instrumental in laying the foundation of awareness among the workers in and around Providence district.

'Thank you,' Hites screamed back. The fact that a truck full of brown workers was being taken to work on Labor Day was enough to upset Hitesbhai. 'Today should be holiday for them.'

'A herd is never on holiday, Red Lady. You know why? Because a herd is always on holiday,' Steve said. He made sense. Every day was a question of existing as an expat—ready to provide labor at any price. But what else could one do in this country anyways, some managers said. They said every day is a holiday in paradise, you need work, you need more work, to be occupied, to be busy, to be worthwhile! So work was great for the subcontinental migrants who had already been through extraordinary rigor and exploitation—they were ready to do the bulky dirty work at lesser cost, with lesser provisions, and lesser rights. The best part was that most did not even know this.

A regiment of workers scattered at the back like pieces of shark on their pick-up truck. This analogy took control of Hitesbhai's thoughts as they moved further uphill. He had no idea of the long tragic journey that Reken had undertaken from one ocean to another. She could bear several boat invasions in the reef but when she witnessed her kin being captured and mutilated—only to be dropped back into the water with fins removed—she experienced horror. Half the community had fallen victim to rampant brutal finning. They would be bled with ferocious cuts and due to the inability to swim after losing their fins, they would immediately sink down to the seabed drowning helplessly. Reken saw her tribe drift below—struggling, paralyzed and sometimes already dead. The idea of escape dawned on her when she was already hundreds of miles away from home. She realized she had been swimming for weeks traversing waters unknown.

Reken had made a long sub-continental sail against the seasonal winds that blew from the poles towards the equatorial region where her home lay. She was a distressed shark on the run for a month swimming from anywhere to anywhere in the southern Atlantic. When she regained some decent shark sanity, she found herself just off the cape. She was at the tip of the continent that let humanity take birth and evolve to conquer all the land so that one day there would be enough of them to take over the oceans too.

Reken stayed near the cape for some time as she found the waters perfect to hunt and mate, if possible. To her diet of human refuse and expired meats, was added some more exquisite continental garbage: cartons of spoilt sausages and wasted cereals from the veld country that would be discarded at the ports. The supply lines had been disrupted during the coronavirus pandemic and so an enormous amount of food shipment was rendered unfit to export.

Reken had no idea about what went on above her dorsal, but she might have been grateful to the virus for seeking natural revenge and enabling a constant supply of food from her tormentors. She swam cautiously for months—avoiding nearby fishing and finning traps—and ate heartily along the coast of the rainbow nation. The oceanic currents provided further comfort to her, though their arrival and departure became highly irregular causing some distress in the refugee fishes that had arrived at the cape just like Reken.

It was an anxious underwater relief camp around the cape. There were fish, crustaceans, krill, and even masses of plankton who had either escaped catastrophes or drifted with the unpredictable patterns of fishing steel boards. They were familiar with human movement due to their unpleasant encounters, but were willing to adapt and survive as they could. Reken hunted in these camps and ripped and chewed strangers lost in distant waters. A stressed animal feeding on stressed animals did not signify a healthy state of affairs at the cape, but it was warm and welcoming enough for innocent beasts to be reassured.

And then the shipping lines resumed. Steel boards flooded the cape. There was danger at every inch and some corals could not even witness sunlight for days as the surface of water was a traffic jam of boats. Darkness replaced the vibrance of the coastal underwaters. There was an ominous silence in the environs. Reken felt her tummy rumbling for days. Occasionally, an eerie tone of shrill from afar seemed to be registered among the crabs on the seabed. And in a few days the crabs left. It was highly suspicious for everyone—they thought the crabs knew about something they didn't. And one day, it became clear: when a killer tribe turned up from nowhere and attacked a group of anchored boats just a few miles off the cape: the orcas were back!

VII

REKEN WAS STRUCK by a hypnotic wave of nonchalance the moment she entered the waters of the Seychelles. Weeks of escaping natural and manmade predators had made her resign to her fate which had taken her to an archipelago somewhere in the Indian Ocean. It was a country without a map—simply because it did not have enough land to be seen above water in a single frame. One could only manage a few dots on a sheet of paper. There were supposed to be a hundred and fifteen dots, but no one knew exactly where to put them while attempting to make a copy. Any two versions of these numerous attempts did not align and thus having a comprehensive map of the country seemed impossible. It was all blue, mostly—unless one just stuck to having a map of the main island where almost all the countrymen lived: Mahé.

Reken had averted threats for days and when she traversed into this blue for the first time, it was as if she had given up finally. When the orcas had arrived at the cape, they attacked the ships first and then went on a rampage of sharks and dolphins. It was an unprecedented day of massacre underwater. The orcas seemed to be under a mysterious spell of anger. They came for hitting the anchored steel boards like kamikaze fighters. A few men fell overboard and a few boats capsized. This fury was unknown. A hot-headed tribe of orcas couldn't be dealt with by any capable force at the cape. And so the wave of violence swept the southern coast of the continent—across several nautical blue waters' ships went down, buoys ripped, jetties destroyed, and check posts disappeared. Reken swam for her life.

Reken swam in such a bout of fear that she felt like diving and surfing towards the horizon with eyes closed. She was hit and injured by a long queue of vessels coming her way along the Mozambique channel. It did not occur to her that perhaps a war had broken out in the Gulf that lay at the end of her journey since she had never known war—and human lives had only perturbed her in a stranger inexplicably tortuous manner rather than directly pillaging her habitat. Yes, she had been forced away from home. Yes, her family and community had been irretrievably disrupted. However, she believed that this was done to her because she was different—she wasn't human. *For humans would never do such a thing to humans,* she thought and kept going.

She was wrong. Humans were doing it to humans. The blood being spilt in the Gulf couldn't reach the edge of Madagascar but an instinctive feeling told Reken to change direction from there. She moved towards the Aldabra atoll where her favourite delicacy awaited her: islands full of tortoises and waters full of sea turtles. She hunted for days and ate so much that it got her dizzy. The steel boards that had been lining up earlier along the way avoiding the tensions near the Suez route seemed to be disappearing from Reken's sight as she kept venturing further away from the coast. This is when she had the first craving for human flesh. It was an epiphany—a moment of gastro-enlightenment. Fear had finally left her body and the air of nonchalance that the archipelago had brought onto her made her feel invincible—once again. 'She was the Ghost of Saint Helena after all,' she remembered. Her graceful teeth and playful fins cut through the warm salty waves that very poignantly moved through the calm surface of Seselwa waters. The stage was set for a gruesome epic—she looked for human prey: not only for gluttony, but revenge!

The Seychelles had always been a sanctuary. All endangered life rushed to it seeking a safe haven—mostly temporary—until things got better for their return. Pirates of the Middle Ages did this, to park their ships at calm natural ports waiting out the violent monsoon to pass. European explorers did this, Vasco da Gama hung out in these islands contemplating his ambitious spice journey to the Malabar and so did the Italian cartographers who were the first to painstakingly include these dots in their maps. French and British colonizers did this, to save themselves from each other during continuous war. Deserting soldiers during the world wars did this: to run away and hide at a more peaceful part of the world. Post-war exiles did this, to flee political arrest and assassinations in their home countries. Modern financial fraudsters did this, to hide their embezzled fortunes and unaccounted wealth—just like erstwhile pirates. Reken was a pirate too! She had sailed across dozens of seas and the safer waters had now welcomed her. But like a pirate, she wasn't satisfied with that alone. Blood was on her mind. She desired to rip apart a man and gulp his insides. *That would be a closure for this transcontinental ordeal*, she thought.

After days of loitering and feeding on terrific red snappers and grouper fish, she spotted a lonely trawler off Astove Island. As she made her way swiftly towards the boat, she recalled the stint of carefree living that the past few days had introduced her to. She wondered why couldn't she be happy with just red snappers, groupers and tuna for the rest of her life. After all the atrocities she had to face to reach a safer reef that she could dominate in an entirely different ocean, was this predatory sprint to gobble a human worth it? The dilemma had reached the tip of her dorsal fin that now banged the edge of the hull of the fishing boat. They knew she was here for them. But so were they.

Within seconds the side nets were pulled and the ropes rolled upwards. The claw lever attached to the trawler was steered towards the deck and there she was: a fierce beautiful tiger shark—gasping and shocked.

'I told you I saw her a few days back,' cried out the young black boy punching the shoulders of the captain of the boat who happened to be his uncle, 'I told you we could get her!' Reken heard his screams of joy and fluttered flabbergasted.

The uncle nodded and wept holding the nephew's arms. 'The Lord has been kind. It has been ages since we caught one of these. We must take it home and have a big feast. The whole village would be so pleased.'

'No no, *abti*! We can't eat this one!' the boy said, 'she is too important to be eaten. We can sell her and have a fortune. The village can have a bigger feast that way.'

'But she is a blessing from god! How can we sell her? And even if we sell her, no Somali will give a good price for her.'

'My poor *abti*! We will not take her back home. We can sell her to these white men on bigger ships. They will pay us in euros. And we can get a better price on the black market.'

The Uncle froze in thought for a few seconds and then agreed. European ships had been fishing in their waters and making the natural catch go dry. Fisherfolk from Eastern Africa had to sail far beyond to be able to bring back some respectable catch to not only feed their families but affirm their masculinity. Many of them never returned — being attacked by pirates or just jumping ship to escape. A bunch of euros would be a good deal, he thought. He asked his nephew to get the wooden bat ready for Reken's body that now hung nearly cold. 'I will slam her eyes myself!'

His eyes shot up as Hitesbhai's head banged against the wooden headrest of the seat. Steve giggled at his sleeping beauty passenger princess who was out on a sunny day to raise a revolution against the most powerful person of the country but was too tired to make the journey uphill even in a pick-up truck—that she wasn't even driving. Red Lady sat up and scratched his stubble. He had been dreaming of the housekeeping lady at the Waro House and now awake he thought of what would he say to her at the gate.

'Mr Beny Waro please… I have brought him the papayas… and the shark cubes… err… I want to meet him… to wish him on Labor Day…as our boss… yes… I know he likes his special feast on first of May every year… so I thought… if it is possible to see him… I would just like to… all the workers have a message for him… oh it will take him time to come… no problem I can wait… or I can come inside if that is okay… I can help you in making the *chutney*… no I have never made it but I would like to learn … yes…

you are very kind madam… you are very nice… you are beautiful too… I wish we could meet before … yes we see each other every Sunday but that is just with Steve I mean… yes Steve is great… but just maybe if we had said hello before… because I am leaving for another island next week… yes for my renewed contract… not just me… all of us at Gangwani… you don't know where Gangwani is?... You must visit us someday… when do you get your days off?... I also work on Sundays like you… yes, it is not fair… we need our holidays… and social security and mobile data… because that is so expensive here… at my home phone bill is cheap… do you have a phone madam?... maybe you can give me your number… no no, it's okay if you don't want to… I just thought I could make some small talk while waiting… before I met Mr Waro… it is very important for me… for all of us workers actually… I can help you make the shark *chutney*… or I can make the papaya salad while you make the *chutney*… these are some great Red Lady papayas… yes, they ripened today suddenly… maybe God wanted me to meet you today… I mean to meet Mr Waro… because it is very important you see… our lives depend on what I have to say… thank you for bearing with me… it is hard to continue like this here madam...'

'*Bainchod*!' his mind screamed and shattered the train of thought. *This beating about the bush won't work*, he thought, *my English won't last that long—I need to come to the point quickly. The four points and the request to meet Waro! The demand! Yes, the demand to meet Waro! The urgency—to meet Waro! The absolute necessity to meet Waro! Now! Then! Now! There! Here! Now! Yes!*

'Are you ok, Red Lady?' asked Steve, 'You seem to be…'

Hitesbhai broke into a sudden unexpected puke. The truck came to a halt and Hites vomited his guts out. Steve patted his back. 'There. It's ok. It can't be the hills today,' he said. The dizzying road had never affected Hites this way. He was fine on every Sunday delivery. 'You must be nervous. It's okay. Waro makes everyone nervous.' Steve imagined what would Waro look like if they did eventually see him: a giant white man in a black suit with piercing eyes and neatly combed golden hair spiking from the left like an orca in captivity—with a spiked dorsal. He would certainly be a ferocious orca in a glass cage. He'd be accompanied by his armed bodyguards, he thought, perhaps the most advanced rifles imported from Russia or the Gulf—the ones that could not be seen anywhere else in the country.

'You worry for nothing. He won't even agree to see us,' he kept patting Hites, 'he would never have an appointment with a Malba.'

Hitesbhai looked at Steve with a frown that made him realize his mistake. Steve apologized and gave the angry Malba his plastic bottle of water. Hitesbhai sipped a sip and wiped his face. 'How much longer?' he asked.

'You know how far, Red Lady! Like every Sunday. Thirty more minutes. We just need to pick up some bilimbi on the way from Marie-May.'

'Today's Wednesday,' said Hitesbhai throwing the bottle back in the trunk and the wheels rolled further uphill.

The plastic bottle rested on the salted shark cubes. It was a sight showing the absolute vulgarity of the modern food chain. Reken had developed an appetite for plastic over the years and now her, food lay on top of herself in the form of food for the same man who owned plastic making industries. She was food for someone who fed her for years something that she wasn't supposed to eat. It was a *chutney* of food webs that disrupted the natural flow of nutrition across the animal kingdom. The sole wild animal of the island kingdom was at Waro House awaiting his May Day feast.

Chetty Papa had taught Hitesbhai how to make the creole papaya salad. It was fairly simple: sautéing grated papayas and adding lime, pepper, and salted onions according to taste. However, due to his love for ripe Red Ladies, he had never tried to make papaya salad. He would enjoy delivering and devouring them as fruit. Bilimbi was another interesting creole fruit—unlike the papaya, it was of little use after ripening. Its magic existed only when plucked green from the tree branches. A cross between starfruit and cucumber, it was mildly sour—a perfect ingredient for the creole *chutney*—the *satini*!

The shark *chutney* was a local delicacy Hitesbhai never bothered about. His vegetarian diet kept him miles away from pondering over its contents or recipe. It was only after hearing Steve talk about picking up bilimbi that he asked him about its use in *Satini Reken*. That was a nudge enough for Steve to tell Hites the entire recipe for Shark *Chutney*.

A good *chutney* is a paradox: dry from the outside and succulent from the inside. It all depends on how well the shark cubes have been juiced dry: first a quick boil of the cubes makes them warm and juicy, and then they are squeezed and dried to be made as mushy as possible. Then comes the most important part for the texture of the shark—flaking. The mushy cubes are flaked and scrambled to take away leftover moisture and even some harmful impurities that may be lying hidden in the linings of the flesh beneath the skin. A well-flaked shark would most certainly make a good *chutney*. Then some bilimbi is grated, salted and added to the flake while keeping the same principle in mind: juice it dry! Like desiccating a salt farm, moisture is removed from the mixture.

At this point, Steve and Hites had reached Marie-May's. She had kept a small sack of bilimbi hanging at the gate. Steve didn't even have to stop the truck. He steered a little towards the left and plucked the bag from the gate and into his lap and drove ahead. He passed the sack to Hites and asked him to have a look at how succulent the fruit felt.

'Then comes the oil, the turmeric, and the onions! Like the Malba curries, Red Lady. You know that.'

'*Tadka*?' Hites asked.

'Yes, *tarka*. Heat the oil on the pan, stir some sliced onions with pepper and turmeric. Put the shark-bilimbi flake into it and warm it up. Add some seasoning and lime juice and voila! That's your shark *chutney*. Simple. Delicious. Genius. Creole!'

Hitesbhai inhaled the fresh bilimbi wrapped in a plastic bag inside the sack. *Almost all things on the island came wrapped in plastic—from fruits to drugs,* he thought.

'Shark *chutney*, papaya salad, mango salad. We keep it simple and fresh. That's the best thing about creole cuisine, Red Lady! No overcooking, just like no overthinking! Relax!'

Steve was right—in fact they kept it way simpler than that. Let alone overcooking, very few cooked at home. Chips and cola were the staple breakfast of an average Seselwa now. An oily chicken curry in starchy rice was lunch from a takeaway shack and dinner would be a carton of ice-cold beers gulped along with fried chicken. There were no food joints in the country except a Burger King at the airport. The well-to-do could go for family buffets on weekends where they would relish an assortment of traditional creole cuisine in which everyone still took immense pride: octopus curry, shark *chutney*, mango salad, tuna steak, red snapper, poulet curry, and black pudding. This would be followed by the extremely sweet coconut nougat and banana cake with *la daube* oozing fragrance of local plantain and honey. A coconut milk toddy would settle things after lunch and the island would be left to the natural flow of wherever the breeze would like to take it.

Despite its humble makeup, Shark *Chutney* was absolute gourmet for the wealthiest too: Waro ate it once a year. Community kitchens made it only during festivals and the tourists sometimes even missed it for other regular dishes like octopus curry, catch of the day and aubergine fritters. Very few could ever be exposed to the philosophy of this recipe—least of all poor trapped Reken, who breathed her last looking at the wooden bat of the Somalian abti onboard his trawler. *Abti* smacked the life out of Reken as his nephew held the net. She was dead before the bat landed on her eye ball.

A bigger frigate could be seen on the horizon. *Abti* and the nephew smiled. Their euros were coming. They both had never tasted a spoon of shark *chutney*—and they did not care. They knew they had killed a tiger and that was enough to make them feel like they had eaten one. That was the philosophy of shark chutney: the fiercest of beings could be had by the meekest. Reken could never know this. She saw her killers. But she could never see her consumers.

3

THE CHUTNEY

VIII

A WEEK AFTER Hittalbhai went back to India to get his deadly wounds nursed—never to return—Hites raised a call for protest among the worker folk. He took Chetty Papa and the Gangwani men into confidence first. It was a matter of dignity, he told them, as they all sat huddled together at the back of Steve's pickup, stuck in a painful traffic jam near the Seychelles International Airport. The airport was a colonial legacy, the traffic was its long-term consequence. It was an endless queue that stretched from one end of the island to the other. Incessant rains had lashed Mahé making the sea level rise with the incoming monsoon. Some parts of the east coast road were submerged and the country had come to a halt on the highway.

An island that was used to living slowly did not mind this sudden pause at all. Chetty Papa told the men how they must worship the rain gods. 'If it weren't for these rains, the fire that had broken out because of the blast on the seventh would have devoured everything,' he said, his moustache sprinkling the water droplets landing from the tarpaulin cover that the Gangwani passengers held taut as a collective raincoat on the truck. Everyone hummed in agreement. They knew how efficiently the fire fighters fought fire on the island—first the roaring landfill fires, then the terrifying industrial blast and more recently, the gas attacks being reported by an unknown group called 'The Syndicate.'

'You don't need to fight fire if you are surrounded by all the water in the world,' Chetty Papa said, 'we must raise the fire safety issue at the protest too.'

Hites nodded and affirmed that the protest will focus on the four demands: S.A.C.H! Safety came first in the precedence of the acronym as well, and to further emphasize on its importance it was decided that the protest would be held right in front of the blast site in Providence district. All workers in the district would be communicated the time of assembly and what to bring along. Hitesbhai quickly drafted a message and sent it to all the men seated around him holding the tarpaulin cover from one hand. They forwarded the message to other worker acquaintances from the other hand. And so it was done: the date had been decided, the venue had been fixed, the participants had been invited.

Now all they had to do was wait.

After this momentary excitement of planning, a lull ensued under the tarpaulin. Everyone looked at each other and quietly listened to the downpour. An hour passed in the stagnant pickup. Some of them began to play a game of identifying cars stranded next to them in the traffic jam. There were Fords and Toyotas and Suzukis in the crowd. Towering over them were tall Ashok Leyland and Tata state transport buses. And just beside their pickup—in the special lane on the right—a prancing horse: Ferrari, a raging bull: Lamborghini and an inverted shark fin: Tesla.

'What are these cars made of? They always shine … even in this rain,' Hitesbhai asked Chetty Papa.

'I don't know what they are made of,' he replied, 'Certainly not tarpaulin.'

Eighteen people turned up for the protest at the given time and place: five o'clock just after work—at the blast site. The Gangwani men stood on that solitary road and discussed whether their choice of logistics was bad. They couldn't have held the protest during the day as it would have blocked the only road in the area causing inconvenience to people. 'We have to make the owners and the managers and the contractors hear our problems. We have no fight with the common people,' Hitesbhai said. 'There is no one here right now,' Chetty Papa said, 'but we must raise our slogans no matter.'

Three more men from the neighbouring compound arrived an hour later. They said they had a message from their company requesting the protest to be shifted to some other place. 'A protest will never work here. Look around you.' They were correct. It was a deserted place beneath a beautiful pink sky with a setting sun. The men nodded and stopped their already exhausted sloganeering. A strange calm took over as everyone lay down on the road enjoying the evening breeze. Twenty-one men lying on the road looked at purple candy clouds above.

The sound of an approaching pickup disrupted the peace. It was Steve. 'Papa! I got a media guy!' He had a journalist accompanying him.

'Is this the protest that was to happen?' he asked.

'This is it. We are protesting,' said a cloud gazing banana.

'Interesting!' the journalist remarked and clicked some photos on his iPhone. 'I can't promise you the newspaper.

But I'll put this up on Gossip Corner. That should get you guys into the news.'

He clicked some photos of the sky too—which made it to the front page of the next day's newspaper. There was no news about the protest in the paper but he had posted the photos on the facebook gossip group as promised. The post received ten likes and five comments. The likes were from the Gangwani men themselves—who felt accomplished in some way, but were too confused and unsure of commenting.

The Art-loving Politician commented: 'They are taking our jobs and now they are blocking our roads also! Out with outsiders! Beautiful sky btw! Like a painting! Love it!'

The Religious Headmaster had commented: these restless souls must find faith in faith. May God give them good thoughts. Save our people oh lord!

The Local Ecologist had commented: 'What are their demands? Why is this not in the papers? We must hear them out. They work for our good!'

The other two comments were 'nic pic' and 'k' by Paul Gaming and Sanju Pandya respectively.

After a week, Hitesbhai and his colleagues announced another protest—this time in the heart of Victoria. The plan was to protest near the Clock Tower without disturbing the moving traffic during the day. They would all complete their farm chores early that day and report at the Clock Tower at lunch time in Steve's pickup. 'This would show that we don't stop work even when we have complaints,' Chetty Papa stated, 'Waro would respect us for that. He would take note.'

The Gangwani men did as planned. However, on reaching the Clock Tower they saw two groups already protesting on two corners of the public square. One of the groups was shouting slogans against poisoning of stray dogs that the authorities thought could hurt the tourists on the island and the other group was protesting against the Russia-Ukraine war. Hitesbhai and his team sat quietly on the third corner and held placards made by them that morning which read—'S.A.C.H.! Securty, Acomodation, Conection, Holiday!'

The men stood just outside the Liberty House, which was a building that wore many hats. It was the headquarters for finance ministry, the national post office, the electricity and water board as well as the office of duplicate key makers. It was a versatile building that had recently become a venue for expressing discontent in the country. Protests related to rising cost of living, media freedom, Israel-Palestine conflict and even a call for making beer free had taken place at the front porch of the building—as it was the closest to the Clock Tower. All protests had lasted a little less than an hour. There had even been a candle march for war victims—in broad daylight. In that context, the Gangwani protest could be termed as a success as it lasted for a full hour and also got space in the newspapers the next day.

'Workers Demand Disaster Damages and Dignity' read the headline. Waro apparently took note of this and the Waro Company immediately issued lapel pins shaped as a 'W' for all workers to assure them of solidarity. Thousands of Ws were distributed amongst all the workers of the company across all the islands of the archipelago. 'We are being heard,' said Chetty Papa as he smiled and pinned the W to his breast pocket. All the Gangwani men did the same. 'W' meant the Workers had Won! Little did they know that this was the easiest of giveaways from Beny Waro. Steve and

Hites would discover on their next Sunday Delivery, hundreds of Ws lying around the Waro House and some even flowing down the hill road and drainage pipes after the rain. The 'W' was a peanut symbol. And it was nothing but cheap plastic moulded at the local warehouse—not even giving it the perceived dignity of metal.

More and more 'W's and their broken versions 'V V's were being collected by the waste trucks in the weeks that followed. Many people even complained of clogged drains due to these plastic lapel pins. A month later, a protest against the plastic pins was organized by the Local Ecologist at the Victoria Clock Tower. She roamed around the square for about an hour collecting signatures—most of which turned out to be of white European tourists who left the island in a few days. She submitted the signatures against what she called 'Waro badges' to the environment authority. In the complaint, she also mentioned the unfair treatment of expat labor by the company. Waro's Manager was summoned. And then there was silence for weeks.

Then Chetty Papa was summoned by the Manager—who happened to be from the same ancestral family that had migrated from Mauritius a century ago. Two brown Seychellois Malba sat facing each other at the Waro Head Office. Chetty Papa was given clear instructions to 'Make your people behave.' 'My people?' he had asked. 'Yes, your people,' the Manager replied.

'They are sending you all to another island before monsoon this year.' When Chetty Papa disclosed this to the Gangwani men after his meeting with the Manager, they were confused.

'But all our contracts are expiring in May,' said Hitesbhai.

'Yes. That is why you all have two options. If you want to extend the contract, you go for the construction of a new hotel on the Esomption Estate or the contract simply ends and you all go back home.'

'And what about here?'

'Some new people will come. For lesser money.'

'And what about our demands?'

'There are no demands. The Manager said you can go home if you want to. No security refund in that case.'

'But if we want to work on an island far away, we should be given basic facilities.'

'He said you are living in a paradise. Be grateful.'

It was simple and direct—and quite plausible. The Gangwani men thought about their options. None of them wanted to go back home. Even though they missed home, things were much worse for them there. They missed their families but the anxiety of feeding them made their falsely mistaken 'masculine' shoulders shudder. Fearful frames of hope, money, responsibility, judgement, and hard labor flashed in their eyes as they all kept quiet.

Chetty Papa too, lost in thought, recalled the Manager's words, 'The blast did not happen from any fault of ours. In fact, we ourselves are the victims. We might never know how it happened. It was an accident. Accidents happen everywhere. There is no question of damages or rights here. You don't see anyone else protesting. Why? Because they are not as ungrateful as the shameless Gangwani gang. All you do all day is grow fruits and vegetables. I would love to do that all my life! Be thankful for that comfort. We are giving everything to these people and their families back home. What else do they want in a foreign country! Tell them to have some respect!'

Respect was something they had not been quite lucky with on either side. The dignity of work that they had at home was not encouraging, and the dignity bestowed on them in a foreign land was negligible, but understandable. But a simple demand for rights was the least they could do in life, Hites repeated to the group. A meeting was called on Sunday under the tallest Red Lady tree of the Gangwani Estate and it was unanimously decided that the men would extend their contract, however, they would continue to voice their demands to ensure a better survival on the other island. This would be done through a representative without the Manager knowing. That representative would be Hites, who would try to directly talk to Beny Waro. And so the series of Sunday Deliveries turned into Sisyphus' attempts to roll up papayas to the top of the hill in a hope to meet god.

'You are our hero, Red Lady!' was the last thing he would hear before Steve's pickup accelerated out from the estate every Sunday morning.

'*Bonzour! Komo cava?* Happy May Day, my friends,' Beny Waro's housekeeping lady was right at the gate of the Waro House waiting for Steve. This was it. They had reached. Hitesbhai could not believe that the moment had come. Even though he had done this a hundred times before on a Sunday, reaching this way on a Wednesday made him feel unsure and scared. Images, reflections, and dreams of Beny Waro hijacked his mind. He was to meet a myth today. But first, he must ask.

'I did not expect him to be here,' the lady told Steve referring to Hites.

'Oh, the Red Ladies have ripened, so…' Steve said.

'Yes! I heard about it. Oh lord! How has it come to this now? Is it a sign of a storm coming for this island?'

Steve shrugged and pushed Hites ahead. He had completely zoned out—lost in fear and self-doubt. His feet were cold and his forehead burning.

'And Reken?' she asked.

'Of course. There she is,' Steve said pointing at the back of his truck. A faint smell of the salted cubes of the shark could be sensed from the gate now. The lady smiled. Steve handed over the pieces to her and asked Hites to take the sack of papayas. Hitesbhai was still frozen. He wanted to disappear.

He thought of all other workers who could be there in his place. He did not want to be a hero. He could sense the crushing hand of authority coming at him at the gates of power. He repulsed his own courage which would be seen as audacity of the highest order by Beny Waro. How dare he think of breaching this line? How dare he think of even asking admission into Waro House? Was he even worthy of doing this? What about the other Gangwani men? Isn't there a better representative than this inexperienced, naïve arrogant man who thinks he knows what he is doing?

Hitesbhai's mind had slid downhill all the way to the beach looking for alternatives for a better 'representative.' What were the others doing at this time when he was gulping his own puke to be able to at least voice a genuine concern? Perhaps someone else should have been here, he thought, to face this insurmountable load of humiliating realization of being a nobody. He had never even spoken to the headman of his village back home and now he was standing at the gates of heaven to bargain with the god of a hundred islands!

From his mind's eye he looked for his comrades. Chetty Papa must be going to Victoria to purchase the lottery tickets for the weekend. Breadfruit and Passionfruit might be discussing which football club to bet on this weekend. Bilimbi and Mango might be coming back from the Barrel Bar after spending a night drunk dancing to local tunes of sega and moutya. Frisiter must be in a fight with the pimp near Perseverance. And the Bananas must all be half-drunk at the Casino pulling sticks of slot machines out of hope and boredom at the same time. They must be all over the island right now having a good time, he thought, it is indeed paradise. *The problem is that there are no problems here*, he murmured to himself, *we are just so ungrateful. How horrible of us!*

As Hites hyperventilated, his eyes fell on the shark cubes again making him realize that it wasn't Sunday, it was Wednesday which meant all the Gangwani workers were at the estate working their asses off—May Day meant nothing for them. And that is why he stood at the gate today, he reminded himself, to make the Day count!

'So, I think you can give me the Red Ladies and…' the housekeeping lady said trying to make eye contact with a frozen Hites.

'I want to meet Mister Waro first!' he blurted out. 'Please.'

IX

HITESBHAI SOMERSAULTED IN the eternity between his 'please' and the housekeeping lady's reply which was—to his surprise which lasted another eternity—'Yes of course. Come in please. Follow me.' The lady ushered in a nervous, sweating man, a dead shredded shark, and some sweet Red Ladies inside Waro House. Steve gaped at this as he sat back in the driver's seat wondering if this was the last time he was ever seeing Hites. He pictured him being chewed and digested by an orca in no time and then pondered of how long would it be ethical for him to wait for Hites to come back out of the House.

Beny Waro was not an orca. He was standing right there in front of Hites when he entered with the housekeeping lady. But since Hites had never seen an orca, he was in no condition to make any hurried judgements. In fact, on first glance Hitesbhai noticed that Beny Waro did not look like any animal at all. He did not resemble anyone or anything he had seen before.

Beny Waro wasn't large, he was rather spacious. He wasn't tall, but appeared unreachable. His face wasn't blunt, but seemed ambiguous. His eyes were green—the only sharp feature noticeable. But on a second glance, they looked sort of blue to Hites. They were in fact, emerald but Hites did not know of that color. He had a smile molded by his lips that somehow did not seem to know their place—at first glance they were between his pale cheeks and then they were somewhere close to his falling ears. He was slim till the chest and fat from the waist which rendered his body crooked in a way that one could never know if he were sitting or standing. His overall physiognomy resembled that of an idol in a local temple. Hites could see why Waro was known as the god of the islands. He looked like a marble mass of mysterious power. His skin was so white that when sunlight fell on him, he disappeared for a few seconds. Hitesbhai blinked and joined his hands to greet Beny Waro.

Hitesbhai heard Beny Waro say something, but it wasn't him. Like for a statue, it was hard to know if Waro was saying something or not. His eyes kept gleaming, skin kept glowing and lips kept changing. Hitesbhai was in awe of Beny Waro's appearance for an entire minute—after which he just found the aura disgusting. He had to come to terms with the fact that Beny Waro was quite nauseous to look at. Hites turned his head to the ground and kept it that way thereafter.

Beny Waro was pleased with this show of respect. He acknowledged Hitesbhai's gesture of bowing by a slight wobbling of his chin. 'So you are the gardener for today. Good. Come.' Hites assumed that this voice had come from the breathing statue in front of him that masqueraded as God. Indeed, it had. Beny Waro walked and Hitesbhai followed him head down.

They walked about fifty yards and reached a flagpole standing erect in the middle of a freshly cut grass patch. 'This is where we start. You can see there are nine holes as far as one can see. But since today is a special holiday for May Day, I will only do tee off practice.'

Hitesbhai looked up and a bedazzling sight got hold of him—the most exquisitely green land he had ever seen in his life. As a salt farmer on brown and golden sands of Kutch, he had only seen a lush green countryside in his dreams. Then suddenly, he felt disappointed—seeing that there were absolutely no rows of crops or trees even on a small part of the humongous swathe of land. He looked beside him and Beny Waro was invisible in sunlight—which made him feel like he was in a dream. But he wasn't. In fact, this was the first time in his life that Hites was witnessing a golf course.

As he couldn't see Beny Waro for some time because of the glare, Hites turned to the housekeeping lady and thanked her for letting him in. 'I thought I will never be allowed inside like everyone else.'

'Like who?' asked the housekeeping lady.

'Like everyone … outside,' Hites said fumbling, 'Every Sunday I kept thinking how to come in.'

'You just needed to ask,' the lady said. Hites tried to thank her again but was interrupted by Beny Waro who was back suddenly with a golf club and a golf ball.

'You are my caddie for today, gardener!' he said, flipping a 'W' cap onto his head that had sparse but long hair just above a horrifying forehead. Hites kept looking at the ground and nodded.

'No, not a caddie actually. I just have one club and one ball. So you will be a ball boy. Not a caddie. Understood?'

'Sir there is some mistake,' Hitesbhai replied, 'I am here to talk about something.'

'This might be your hundredth visit to my house, gardener. We will talk about everything over lunch. We have a lot of time. Today is a holiday. Relax. You will have the best shark *chutney* ever.'

Hites was visibly perturbed by the proposition, 'Sir, no non-veg. Only vegetarian sir.'

Beny Waro looked closely, 'Eggs?'

'No sir. Veg only.'

'Are you from Mandvi?'

'You know Mandvi, sir?'

'Victoria was built by people from Mandvi. All you Shahs and Dhanjis and Raghwanis and other vegetarians from Kutch. All my old friends. Haven't seen them for ages now. They probably hate me.'

'I am from a village far from Mandvi but in Kutch only sir,' a delighted Hitesbhai said, 'your friends are big rich caste people sir. I am from a small salt-farmer family.'

'Okay. You see this ball?' Beny Waro bounced the golf ball on his palms and placed it in between his thumb and index finger, 'It looks like a frozen fistful of white salt, doesn't it? I will hit it down this green farm of mine and you will get it back for me to hit it again. Got it?'

Hitesbhai glanced at the overwhelming size of the golf course and an unsettling chill of weariness went through him.

'After we are done with this labor of an exercise, we will have a nice lunch. I will have the *chutney* and you can have your papayas. Sounds good?'

Hites didn't seem to have anything to say to that. He quietly looked on as Beny Waro took his position next to the tee and drove a hearty club hitting the ball as hard as he could. The white ball disappeared in the white sky—

momentarily—like Waro in sunlight. Hitesbhai spotted the ball as it dropped hundreds of yards away. He knew he had his task cut out: to run downhill and get the ball back up. He took a deep breath and removed his slippers.

'Run!' whispered the housekeeping lady from behind.

Hitesbhai felt alone and isolated that afternoon as he did a hundred rounds of running downhill to get the golf ball uphill for Beny Waro to tee off yet again. He was missing Steve and his pickup as he was reminded of every single Sunday Delivery that he had done in the past two years. He wondered how did Beny Waro know that this might be his hundredth visit to Waro House—but with every successive round, it became clearer to him how closely Beny Waro kept an eye on all his workers on the island.

Each time Hitesbhai put the golf ball on the tee nailed to the ground, Beny Waro made a few unrelated statements to which Hitesbhai nodded before running downhill again:

'You are lucky to be young, to be able to run, to look forward to the future unlike myself—an old man with basic survival needs.'

'Breathe deep before running back, gardener. The others don't do it that fast.'

'I only hire gardeners at my house because my property is just a big lawn as you can see. There are six of them here. Five men and the lady that let you in. She grows avocados here.'

'Avocados are just eggs growing on trees. Avocados can be eggs, but eggs can't be avocados. Like the expat workers here. You all can never be avocados.'

'You like it here, don't you? Less people, clean air, good roads, less crime. You would want to stay here forever rather than going back home to your dusty farm and nagging families.'

'Be grateful to my company, boy. Thanks to me, you are on these beautiful virgin tropical islands trying to smell some virgins on your own. But you won't find them, so stop focusing on that elusive goal. Women run this country; they are the masters. If they let you in just go for it and enjoy yourself sometimes.'

'You are lucky the Sheikhs didn't take you with them. You will be belted every now and then. And here. Here, there are no rules. So be thankful.'

'Hundreds of you just reach America somehow—only to be kicked back out. Or be jailed for life. Horrible. Here we don't do that because we value you. We know you help build our country. Be glad that you aren't with your brothers swimming to America or Europe. We don't deport, we support.'

'My father and my brothers did a lot for this country. And I am doing my bit. The French came and the British came and there were two hundred years of bare existence, but we did our best to put these islands on the map.'

'We have a serious drug problem and a serious drinking problem in the country. But what is worse is the problem of delusion. People believe they are equal. How can you and I be equal? I throw the ball and you fetch it.'

'To be rich enough to be invisible was my goal, and to stay invisible is my struggle. You are lucky to be seen and forgotten.'

It was on the hundredth round, Hitesbhai would like to believe, that his body was rendered exhausted beyond return. The last visual he remembered was falling on the nail beside Waro's club with all his sweat watering the grass and blinking to the housekeeping lady.

He was spent. A blackout creeped in and took over his consciousness as Beny Waro disappeared yet again—in broad daylight.

X

IT WAS THE smell of bilimbi-smeared smoked shark that woke Hites up. He was taken aback seeing himself at the lunch table with Beny Waro and three strangers. They looked somber and hesitant, as opposed to Waro who was excited to begin his special feast. Hitesbhai tried to look around for a clock; he did not know for how long he had fainted.

'Now that you are back to being yourself, I must introduce you to the guests at the table,' Beny Waro said with gleaming emerald eyes, 'Lady and gentlemen, he is a capable, Brown Salt Farmer who works for me as a papaya grower and now gardener and golf ball boy.'

Hites looked even more confused. Beny Waro turned to the strangers at the table and pointed his fat white ringed fingers at each of them to introduce them to Hitesbhai.

'This is a proud Black Religious Headmaster who gives bible study courses at the Victoria Anglican,' Beny Waro said, 'this is my old Asian Artist friend who has recently turned Politician with the National Development Party and this is a White Local Ecologist teaching at the University of Seychelles down south of the island. And me? You all know me for many things, but all I can say about myself is that I am a Good Creole Seselwa.'

A long pause took its place comfortably at the centre of the pentagon drawn on the table. A star was drawn inside the pentagon joining the five points where each of them sat. It was a roundtable with a pentagon with a star.

'Okay now you can use your phones to record my video message,' Beny Waro said to the three quiet strangers who suddenly took out their phones with extraordinary zeal and began recording the table with their iphones.

Beny Waro began: 'This is to all the workers of my country and the world! Today, I'm having the special May Day feast in your honor like every year, but I am joined by four guests that have made this table a fine assortment of humanity. We are all eating together—black, white, brown, yellow and creole. I know creole is not a color, but it is a rainbow that you get from all colors. We celebrate diversity and hard work done by all of you. And along with the wishes for the day, I must also share a news with you—which is why I decided to make my first public address through social media. The news is that I will be retiring by the end of this year. I have finally made my decision and I think young blood must take my place. So, I want you to send applications and spread this message far and wide. Because anyone can dream of becoming the chair of the Waro Company. It is a transparent, professional, democratic and noble organization that has built this beautiful country for years now. With that, I thank you for listening to me and I hope you have a great May Day like my comrades here who will now relish some home-made Shark *Chutney* with me! Cheers. God bless.'

The three stopped their recording at this juncture and the three beeps from the three phones beeped in unison. 'That was wonderful.' 'Thank you so much for this.' 'This will break the internet.' 'No one has ever seen you like this before.' 'Now they will know how real you are, Mr Waro!' 'So inspiring.' 'So humble.' 'Thank you for your generosity.' 'I will post it on the Gossip Corner right away!' 'Hey, no! Wait! I will post it on the Gossip Corner first!' 'No need both of you. I have already posted it. See!'

Beny Waro looked very pleased—and Hitesbhai still very confused.

The table was an unfamiliar display of familiar entities to Hites. He knew the Shark, but not as *chutney*, he knew the pumpkin but not as salad. Papayas were Red Ladies for sure, but cut in a unique fashion—carved into stars and ducks and wheels. There were pigs as ribs, hens as sausages and cattle as steak. SeyBrew beer and Taka Maka rum were in diamond pitchers while the *pema* chili sauce was kept in a hollowed coconut shell. Everything known had suddenly transformed into something unknown since he had come back to his senses. The three strangers and Beny Waro started eating while Hites continued to look for a clock.

'Why aren't you eating anything? Have your papayas at least!' Beny Waro called out to Hites across the table. Hitesbhai was shaken and his eyes fell straight onto the salt cellar. The familiarity pulled his hand towards it. He grabbed the salt and sprinkled it on his empty plate. Then he pulled out his tongue to wet his thumb which he dabbed onto the salt in his plate and tasted it. The white crystals satiated the out-of-place feeling in him for a while as he heard Beny Waro give a sermon on the table.

'Get me just ten Malba and I will run a successful food delivery business on this island I am telling you,' Waro was saying, 'We people have stopped cooking at home and all that we grab are takeaways for breakfast, lunch, and dinner. The Seselwa need a good food delivery business. But to run that we need a Malba mentality. Of hospitality. To let the customer be god! Because no Seselwa will treat his customer like that. Low charges, less salary, no tips and yet hard working and no complaints. A Malba on a two-wheeler is the most productive thing in the world, no matter what comes in his way—storms, floods, quakes, or bomb blasts.'

'Sir, I wanted to…' Hites mumbled.

'Quiet!' Beny Waro shouted, 'I have been treating you with so much respect and you keep bringing up that topic. I know what you are here for ok! But today is a holiday! I do not talk business. And since I am going to retire and leave this island, you can take it up with my manager afterwards. And when you renew your contract next week, which I know you will, I will see you on Esomption Estate building my goddamn brilliant hotel! You have an unprecedented honor of being here today. Respect that! Don't be like that ungrateful bloody comrade of yours, that rowdy Hittal. See what happened to him for creating such nuisance!'

Hites was scared—but he felt exhaustion more than fear. He kept sucking on the salt and kept his head low to avoid seeing the lips of Beny Waro that were now devouring Reken from the edge of his nose.

'You know why the British and the French sent all the troublemakers to Seychelles? Anyone who was a problem for them was exiled to this place. King Prempeh, the Addus, the Bugandan emperor, Malagasy folks, Chagosians, and even Yaa Asantewaa who tasted the first shark *chutney* from my ancestral kitchen! They were all sent here—because this place guarantees peace. It teaches you that rebellion, revolution, protest or disobedience are unnecessary once you reach paradise. And you have reached paradise. Hittal had reached paradise. But some of you just don't acknowledge that. Do you even realize the air you are breathing is a luxury? It is a blessing for all you Malba! I spit on your thanklessness! I respect your work but what disgusts me is this Malba way of…'

Hitesbhai looked at the fork kept beside his plate. He had been silently counting the number of times Beny Waro uttered the M-word. He was determined that with the sixth utterance of 'Malba' by Beny Waro, revolution would arrive in this country with a fork plucking an emerald (or whatever that shade was) eyeball. He also had plans for the knife which he would use to slice the scalp while pinning the spacious man to the ground. But the sixth utterance did not come. Instead, an inexplicable silence burst out on the table from the centre of the pentagon, or so it seemed.

Hitesbhai lifted his head to see why the boisterous rant had suddenly stopped. He saw something unexpectedly gory—Beny Waro was stuck—choking on the same shark *chutney* he had been delightfully chewing at the table. The three strangers took out their iphones once again—to start a livestream of the occurrence. None of them called the ambulance. They were screaming at the top of their lungs. The Politician, the Headmaster, and the Ecologist shoved their phones into the placid red face of Beny Waro. He was not moving.

Hites was still seated at his chair licking salt to reassure himself that this was real. The housekeeping lady came running and joined the cacophony of screams. Hearing the chaos, Steve came in running too. He was taken aback by what he saw. He couldn't really make out if Beny Waro was a real man or an immobile fleshy effigy placed on the table in the centre of a pentagram drawn to do some *greegree*. The lady asked Steve to get the ambulance. The three strangers jumped: 'I think he is dead.' 'Too late.' 'It all happened so suddenly.' 'The RIP messages have started already on the chat.' 'We must pray for his soul.'

Hitesbhai was still on his chair. He began using the cutlery to serve himself a few pieces of the Red Lady papayas. He wondered how could one choke on shark *chutney*. He had seen it closely and it seemed well-shredded. He thought there might have been something in the bilimbi. And at that juncture he saw Beny Waro's lips. They were sealed with a small plastic hook protruding. Hitesbhai suddenly climbed the table lifting his fork and knife. He reached out for the face and used the fork to hold the slippery lips and the knife to cut and part them. The procedure was being recorded online and a comment appeared immediately: 'We have a hero!'

Hitesbhai stuck the fork right into the front teeth pushing the tongue aside and scooping out the plastic hook entangled in reken shreds. It was a plastic 'VV' lapel pin twisted from the middle: one V had blocked the throat while the other V had gotten hooked to the lips of Beny Waro. Now people online could see what had tried to kill the most powerful man on the island—his own merchandise.

'Hero!' comments kept coming in on the chat and the three strangers changed the panic-stricken screams to a reassuring commentary of 'I think he is still breathing' 'He has come back from the dead' 'This is unbelievable' 'Let's get him to the hospital asap'!

'We can take him in my pickup. It's just outside,' Steve was seen saying on camera. This garnered comments instantly: 'We have another hero!'

Steve took out the truck, the three strangers carried Beny Waro, and loaded him in the back carrier. The Politician remarked, 'It smells strange'; the Headmaster added, 'It smells of fish'; the Ecologist said, 'It smells of shark.'

'Or perhaps an orca,' Steve said as he pressed on the accelerator taking Beny Waro downhill towards the hospital. The three strangers, holding Waro still, continued to vlog the journey as the truck rolled out of the Waro House compound.

Hites sat on the tee-off grass patch with the golf club next to him. He held the plastic lapel pin laced with Beny Waro's spit and shark chutney in his palm. He clutched it, wiped it in grass and kept it on the tee. It looked like the tombstone of Beny Waro. Just that it was placed as an 'M' and not as a 'W'. He knew Waro was dead.

The housekeeping lady was cleaning the table. She also knew that Waro was dead and couldn't stop smiling. Hites noticed that and carried the golf club to the table.

'He had always been good to me,' she said, 'but his passing feels like a release.'

'What time is it?' Hites asked her.

'There are no clocks in the house. The Red Ladies keep the time.'

He nodded and looked at the papayas he had brought for Waro. The lady brought them onto the empty pentagon table. Hites handed over the golf club to her. She took it and smirked—and with as much force as she could gather, she hammered a papaya open. The pulp from the battered fruit flew onto Hitesbhai's face. He licked the red bits and laughed. The lady struck the second papaya as both of them laughed together. There was more pulp for Hites to sickle out from his stubble and cheeks and relish the sweetness. They both continued to laugh. They had no blood on their hands; just papayas on their faces. The best papayas in the world. The papayas of paradise. Beny Waro had been correct—the island was paradise indeed. And they were thankful for being there.

But they preferred home.

DVSK

JONATHAN EXTENDED HIS neck towards the setting sun. Another day had passed without much inconvenience. He would now recede into his shell and sleep quietly till he felt the morning warmth early next day. He was good at it. He had been doing it for years and years. He was a good dreamer too—how else would he have survived a couple hundred years on Saint Helena like that!

As he began to turn back from the shore to crawl towards his resting pen, he noticed a thorn pricking up his left forelimb. He moved aside slowly and saw a W-shaped lapel pin. These had been lying around the whole estate after the Christmas party. Jonathan had been collecting these and putting them in the bag kept on the shore next to the green trash can. Looking at this latest W under his feet, he realized sleep had to wait. He began moving towards the green trash can.

It took him a few minutes to reach the can. But delirium kicked in when he couldn't find the bag around the can. The bag had been full of Ws and the one W now in his mouth would have no other place to be kept in. His foggy eyes looked left and right but there didn't seem to be any sign of it. It was dark now and the floodlights of the estate were lit suddenly—which made him see some Ws behind the can.

He moved towards the little plastic Ws behind the can and discovered a trail leading towards the shore. This excited old Jonathan. He made his way picking up each W on the way, and finally reached the shore where something out of the ordinary awaited him: a green turtle!

He saw the turtle in the ocean swimming with the plastic bag of Ws. The turtle looked young and agile—he was chewing on the bag as the Ws fell out and around him. Jonathan felt confused. He didn't know how and why the turtle was there, but seeing one again after decades induced a strange bout of nostalgia in him, and his dream of being a turtle someday and swimming back home took shape again right in front of his cataracts.

The turtle disappeared into the depths, releasing a spree of Ws on the surface. Jonathan smiled and hoped for the turtle's safety. That night, Jonathan dreamt of being a shark.

AUTHOR BIO

Vikram Grewal is a diplomat, somewhat by profession and sometimes by nature. He is an essayist and storyteller who runs the popular blog *Besan Ka Halwa* where he writes about books, films, and music. He is the creator of the multilingual online video series *20 Bisous* (2021) and *Moh Maya Mahé* (2023) as well as the author of the book *Essays / P.T.O: A Case Against Writing in Uncertainty (or Otherwise)* (2024). He has worked in India, France, and Seychelles. He harbors mixed feelings for seafood.